Finest Cuts
Best of the first five years

Razur Cuts
Finest Cuts: Best of the First Five Years

Published by Razur Cuts Books (2021), a subsidiary of Nameless Town

Individual work © The Contributors

All rights reserved. No part of this publication may be reproduced, stored in a retrieval system, or transmitted, in any form or by any means, without the prior written permission of the publisher or individual writer, poet, photographer or artist

razurcuts@gmail.com

ISBN: 978-1-914400-70-4

Edited by Dickson Telfer and Gillian Gardner
Typeset by Dickson Telfer
dicksontelfer@hotmail.com

Cover design by stonedart
stonedart.co.uk

Printed and bound by Martins the Printers, Berwick-upon-Tweed

*To those
who never stopped
believing in themselves.*

INTRODUCTION

After attending an event in Waterloo, London in November 2015, put on by *PUSH*, a literary magazine run and edited by Joe England, the seed was planted in my mind to create a literary, music and arts mag of my own. I felt my home town of Falkirk would benefit from such a thing and was confident I could reach out to like-minded people all over.

Integral to this was the punk DIY attitude, giving a huge nod to the fanzines of the mid to late 70s and using their ethos to promote and help the underground scene. The aim was to include writers, poets, musicians, artists and anyone who'd had good-quality submissions rejected due to elitism. We'd open doors to talent, not close them.

Family and true friends came on board to help and, after almost a year, Razur Cuts was born. Our first edition was released on 30th September 2016 and sold an incredible 280 copies! Since then, we've grown considerably and now have ten issues under our belts.

Showcasing people's art has been exceptionally rewarding for us, so much so that we decided the best way to celebrate five years and ten issues would be to compile an anthology of *Finest Cuts*. We hope you like our choices.

May we take this opportunity to thank everyone who has submitted work to the mag, bought a copy or two, agreed to an interview, or attended any of our events since our incarnation. It's been an absolute pleasure to meet so many of you and become friends.

Razur Cuts is a volunteer-run, independently published, not-for-profit, anti-bourgeois street-lit mag for people who matter . . . without you, we're nothing.

Love to you all.

Derek S
December 2021

CONTENTS

Razur Cuts
Paul Research   18

Issue I front cover
Tam Main   19

Lettres
Tam Main   20

The Grief I Feel
Michaela Hunter   21

Razur Cuts interviews . . .
Ian Rankin   25

Lesbe Friends
Fee Johnstone   32

Shoap
Dickson Telfer   36

London's Calling
Saira Viola   38

Six Million Reasons to Hate
Quirk   39

Razur Cuts interviews . . .
Jean-Jacques Burnel 41

Debt
Mr Mo 45

Why Bother in This Life?
Ella 46

Burnt Orange Peel
Julie Rea 48

Select a Different Religion
Meek 50

Issue III back cover
Andrew Gardner 51

The Orange Dictator
Greig Adams 52

Issue IX front cover
Debs Mullen 53

If Santa was an Immigrant
Hendo 54

The Real Housewives of Tamfourhill
Scott T. Steel 55

A Cultural Guide to Carlisle #1:
The Bin Outside the Train Station
Josh Holton   60

Fitting In
Jared A. Carnie   62

Mourning Potion
Alice Rose   63

Razur Cuts interviews . . .
Big John Duncan   64

The Keychain
Rob Plath   74

Lester McCoy
Helen McGinn   75

Issue VIII front cover
stonedart   76

Hangin Gutties
Colin Dalglish   77

Issue II back cover
Andrew Gardner   78

Remembrance Sunday
Ian Parris   79

Razur Cuts interviews . . .
Tony Drayton — 88

Morning Has Broken
Michael Keenaghan — 95

Jim, One of a Kind?
Ian Bradley — 100

Hello
Kevin Tosca — 101

Razur Cuts interviews . . .
Sleaford Mods — 102

Lane Closed
Jason Williamson — 106

Tattooed Brits on Holiday
Peter McDonald — 108

The Daily Male
J.A. Welsh — 109

Normally
Ian Cusack — 110

Razur Cuts interviews . . .
John Robb — 112

Girl in the RC specs
Derek S — 123

Issue II front cover
Gordon Whyte   124

Planning a Comeback
David F. Ross   125

Action Man Isn't Coming Back
Stephen Watt   126

Razur Cuts interviews . . .
Martin Geissler   128

When It All Kicks Off in Foredyke
Jim Higo   136

Black Flag Kinda Day
Bradford Middleton   138

Searching for Answers
Martin Geraghty   139

Razur Cuts interviews . . .
Richard Jobson   141

Finishing Off
Dickson Telfer   145

The Apprentice
Will B   149

Edinburgh Streetkids
Debs Mullen   153

Barbed Wire Coo View
Gordon Whyte 154

Issue X front cover
Marcel Herms 155

Hot Air Taxi
Heather Scott 156

The Dream is Over
Mark English 157

Wasted Vista, Part 0
Saira Viola 159

Razur Cuts interviews . . .
Paul Research & Suky Goodfellow 160

Thanks, Driver
Sophie McNaughton 165

The Ruts
James McCulloch 170

Birth Certificate
James McCulloch 171

Issue I back cover
Tam Main 172

Issue IV front cover
Scott T. Steel 173

Ventriloquist's Dummy
Gus Rae   174

Find Your Tribe
Johnny Da Silva   175

Gambling
Janet Crawford   178

Razur Cuts interviews . . .
Sons of Southern Ulster
(Justin Kelly & David Meagher)   179

The Girl with The Green Hair
Stuart McIntosh   188

Old Fags
Will B   190

Old Fags
Will B   191

Issue IV back cover
Derek S   192

The Wind & The Rain
Derek S   193

Granite Flats
Tam Main   194

Razur Cuts interviews . . .
JB Barrington 195

Gordon the Traffic Warden
JB Barrington 201

**Self-Destruction II:
Dreams Take My Fight**
Kirsty Allison 203

The Fall
Julian Colton 206

Knavish Tricks to Crush
John Tinney 209

Urinal Cake
Chris McQueer 212

The Pub Bore's Stale Tale
Bobby Gant 214

Razur Cuts interviews . . .
John Zip McNeill 218

Tricks of the Trade
Jared A. Carnie 226

Shadow Wave
Anne Whyte 227

Going Up
Gregor Boyd   228

NATO Base, Berlin
Sean Fitzgerald   229

Skylight
Sean Fitzgerald   230

Razur Cuts interviews . . .
The Moonlandingz   231

Sometimes
Joseph Ridgewell   236

The Truth Walks Alone
Gary Lammin   237

Acknowledgements   238

RAZUR CUTS
Paul Research

Darkly comic, a snarl from the playing field at dusk. The noisy voices you'd cross the street to avoid on the way home, but you're drawn towards on your holiday abroad.

Delivered with a punk staccato, it vibrates the layer of the rust that comes from disuse, it clears its throat and gobs at a pigeon, it sits down and looks at its feet in the dusk. It breaks down in the pub. Then it gets up and laughs again. It has its regrets.

Single serving drama, all the more poignant because who knows when the author might return to haunt you again.

Stamped out fag breaks, watching for the post, an eye on the weather, it heads back inside. Razur Cuts is juggling the everyday blues and getting its LOLs in the shadows and reflections of pound shop windows.

Born of the pre-internet excluded by its nicotine habit, briskly sceptical, flavoured with a dystopian outlook scented with swing park dog shit. Sex behind the pub, depicted by Dali, cheated by a swingers' ad. Self-educated/university of knife.

Verbal fry up, damned for its accent. It flexes its muscles, reaches out and stretches, catches itself in a mirror and thinks: it's not too late yet – is it?

Primed to go viral, preening itself for the digital cloudburst, preserving its energies, biding its time.

Tam Main

Tam Main

THE GRIEF I FEEL
Michaela Hunter

I sometimes hold it half a sin
To put in words the grief I feel:
For words, like Nature, half reveal
And half conceal the Soul within.

Tennyson, In Memoriam A.H.H

Sin. A word I fucking hate. Its meaning has been lost. It's a piece of chocolate on a diet or nasty gossip in a magazine. A sin to me is something shameful. I'll tell you I don't agree with shame, but I feel it. Things run over and over in my mind that I've done, or haven't done. A small knot that unravels as I shut my eyes to sleep. Unknown guilt in my gut swirls. For what, I don't know. Because I didn't do all the things I was supposed to that day. Because I didn't listen. Because there are dirty clothes on the fucking floor. It all builds up till my head is on fire and my spine tightens. Ask me, ask me what's wrong. 'Nothing, I'm just tired,' I'll say.

Sin is the worm in my soul that burrows. I blurt out replies to arguments I had ten years ago, then cover them up. 'Nothing, I was talking to the dog'. But I can't tell you how it makes me feel, I can't explain it. That's good though. No-one wants to hear it. In the grand scale of things, I'm nothing, a nobody. Scraping by. I hold it more than *half a sin* to talk about how I feel. Who would listen?

This is why I write. I put my words in others' mouths. They are not mine, I pretend. I give imaginary people real emotions that I can't deal with. Socially awkward friends to make me feel less alone. I feel something bubble to the surface, but before it gets out I write it in my little notebook – and let a character suffer its magnitude later. Then I lock it away and swallow the key. My gut is full of keys. This isn't cheating. I *put in words* my emotions, I just disguise them with the faces of others. I don't have to feel shame that I'm failing. I don't have to plunge into the depths of my melancholy. Then I can avoid the guilt, or at least some of it, for what the fuck have I got to be sad about?

If it weren't for words, given to paper, what would I do? Sit there, inwardly crumbling. My mind like an infinity mirror and my feelings the flame in front of it. I'd have to reflect, think and reason, then recuperate. I'm not fucking doing that. For the feeling at the top of Everest might be wonderful, but it doesn't make the climb any easier. 'Write down your emotions, then address them. You'll see it's not as bad as you think'. Well, I do. But someone else can address them. I can't.

My mind is a broken leg and my guilt the surgeon that won't fix it. Grief defined is sorrow, caused by someone's death. It's a coil in my mind; push it down and down, don't let it go. But I don't grieve. Every loss I've ever felt, I carry with me every day in guilt. It intensifies and my being slowly erodes. The only loss I grieve, purely grieve, is the loss of me.

Tennyson's words don't belong to me because they show me how to grieve. They're mine because my smile hides anger, sadness, bitterness, I'm not even sure. My face rarely matches my emotional state. I tell you I understand: I don't. I spend hours, days, weeks trying to.

I say that I'm comfortable, at the same time wanting to tear the flesh from my bones. Visitors sit with cups of tea chatting carefree, but I'm counting the seconds till they leave. Touchy feely friends lean in for hugs that I return, whilst recoiling inside. Chatty folks who don't take breaths make me hold my own. Hurt feelings surface at my disappearance from daily life, but I'd rather that than let anyone in. I won't say how *I feel*.

Everyone has something that temporarily fixes them. Even people like me, even just for seconds. For me its forests, the denser the better. Tall trees that appear to have no end. The powerful trunks eager to escape the undergrowth, flowering their beauty. While underneath hides ugly roots that take hold in the ground. They won't be moved. Even when the flowers go, or an axe is taken to the wood, the roots stay there still. Once they rot, they'll always leave a sign that they were there, the ground forever scarred. The soul of the forest is best seen at dusk, for dusk is the autumn of the day and autumn is my favourite season. *Nature* is shutting down. I watch the leaves fall gracefully, envious. That's it for them, their life is over. But there is no kicking and screaming, no reflection, no regret. No clinging on for dear life, no resisting. I revel in the scent of their decay, but shiver at the thought of my own. And then the quick fix is gone. I am the tree, a great mass of ugly roots, hiding.

I can't conceal it all. If they look closely enough, they'll see. My integrity to protect myself won't hide my eyes, glassy. I cannot stop them from seeing me stumble when my body won't keep in time with my brain. The beads of sweat on my forehead look foreign on a cold day. When I ask them to repeat their words or miss their point entirely, I'm rude. That's fine, I'm fine. I'm rude.

My feet give up mid-step and don't belong to me when they hit the floor. Even my muscles lack fucking conviction. She can see it, the physio. When she checks my spine for tension, there is more tension than spine. My body will *half reveal* the inner turmoil of my mind.

My words, my favourite words: I'm fine, *half conceal* the truth of my troubles. Every time my heart thumps in my chest, it reminds me of all I'm doing wrong. It beats too fast. My smile masks a hundred pains in almost every nerve. When I say 'no problem', my mind buzzes with *I can't, I can't, I really can't*. Fear manifests as angry outbursts and irritation, but I'm rude, remember?

This guilt and fear slowly penetrates my being. I am no longer me. She retreated long ago, peering around the corner of my grief, waiting. My *soul within*, weeds of despair choked and tangled. Like a favourite necklace that is knotted beyond repair, but still you keep it in a box, safe. Tennyson's words didn't speak to the person that you see. That minute constricted part of my soul that fights back absorbed his sentiment for the hologram that uses my feet. His words are for the real me and I'll never forget them as long as I live.

Razur Cuts interviews
IAN RANKIN

In January 2021, Razur Cuts (RC) chatted to one of Scotland's most prolific crime writers, Ian Rankin (IR).

RC: **What was life like as a young lad in Cardenden?**

IR: My mum and dad were working class and it was a small, tightly-knit community. Everyone knew everyone else. I was a bit of a dreamer – not good at sports, and not tough enough for the local gang. I became a bit of a chameleon – I didn't want to seem 'different' or 'weird', but I was probably happiest in my bedroom, reading comics, scribbling song lyrics and drawing cartoon strips.

RC: **Did you always receive *Oor Wullie* and *The Broons* books at Christmas? Did you research Dudley D. Watkins on the back of these legendary Scottish comic masterpieces?**

IR: My memory is that in the 1960s and 70s, *The Broons* and *Oor Wullie* took it year about. I was always a bigger fan of the latter. We got *The Sunday Post* each week so those cartoons and the accompanying Merry Mac Fun Page were read religiously! To be honest I had no notion of Dudley D. Watkins or his importance to Scottish culture – not until I was much older.

RC: **When you were working your way through school, was writing always what you wanted to do?**

IR: I was good at English – it was my favourite subject and I loved it when we were asked to write short stories. My teachers were always very enthusiastic and encouraging.

RC: **The days of corporal punishment prevailed then. Did you ever receive the belt?**

IR: I got the belt mostly for talking in class and once or twice for bunking off school. There were some real sadists around in those days.

RC: **What book should be essential on the curriculum in today's world?**

IR: Maybe *1984*. It sometimes seems we are in danger of heading that way.

RC: **Music always comes across as an obsession of yours. Were your formative years Bowie, glam rock or stuff from *Top of the Pops*, possibly prog? How did the punk/new wave explosion change things for you? Is there a band you'd wished you'd seen, but never? And what were the best venues from back in the day?**

IR: The first band I really loved was T. Rex. I was firmly in the T. Rex camp rather than Slade. Never had the suedehead and when my mum was eventually persuaded to buy me a pair of Docs, she got oxblood loafers! Not quite what I had in mind. I loved The Sensational Alex Harvey Band and Status Quo, and dallied with prog rock – Yes, Genesis, and Emerson, Lake & Palmer – without ever really loving it.

Punk was a revelation. Stuart Adamson, guitarist in Skids, was two years above me at Beath High. We used to go see Skids all the time. That punk philosophy – just get up and give it a go – followed me to university. I would try getting my stories and poems published everywhere. Nothing was going to stop me trying.

Bands I wish I'd seen: Frank Zappa/The Mothers of Invention, Hawkwind around 1972-74, The Blue Nile, Cocteau Twins, The Associates . . . The list could run for pages.

Venues: I remember my first ever gig. Barclay James Harvest – a pal was a fan – at the Usher Hall in Edinburgh around 1975/76. I still think that's a great venue. Tim Burgess of The Charlatans asked me to open for them with a DJ set there a few years back, so I finally got to step onto that stage!

RC: **What are your views on the contemporary music scene and the way people listen to and discover new music?**

IR: I'm a bit of an old fuddy-duddy and only recently was persuaded – by the same pal who took me to see Barclay James Harvest all those years ago – to try a streamer. Since buying one, I've been listening to more music than ever. I still buy vinyl, but hardly ever CDs. Musicians had it especially tough during the coronavirus lockdown, so I've been trying to buy as much as I can from Bandcamp etc. T-shirts and merch as well as albums. It's really hard for young bands and musicians especially, but at least the internet and social media gives them a chance to introduce themselves to potential new fans. I subscribe to a few Patreon style things which gives me access to new music, either as downloads or sometimes on vinyl. Last Night From Glasgow is a favourite – and a bargain!

RC: **Were you inspired by Skids, who made local people realise they could be creative themselves, or were you involved in a creative process of your own anyway?**

IR　I remember my school pal Dauve. He invited me to join his new band. This was just after I'd started uni. We were called The Dancing Pigs and we had a plan that Stuart Adamson would produce our first single. Things never got that far, though we did all chip in for a couple of sessions in a professional studio. We were certainly influenced by the success of Skids – though Dauve modelled himself on David Sylvian and wanted us to be Japan. We sent a tape to John Peel, who never played it. I'm told he kept everything though, so we are lurking in his archive somewhere . . .

RC: **This is our obligatory question . . . Is it cheesy toast, roasted cheese, toasted cheese or cheese on toast?**

IR: Cheese on toast for me, with roasted cheese a close second.

RC **Have you ever been in a situation where your thought process or reaction has been that of one of your characters from your stories?**

IR: I give my character Rebus a lot of good one-liners but, alas, in real life situations I only ever think of great comebacks when it's too late to use them. I remember when I was living in London and got burgled. When the police arrived, I showed them how the burglars got in and the footprints I'd found in the back garden, which showed the route they'd taken with all the stuff they'd nicked. I'm not sure they were impressed by this would-be Sherlock Holmes. And the miscreants were never caught.

RC: **How much satisfaction do you get from being involved in your charity work?**

IR: It's pleasing that I have enough spare cash to allow me to chip in to various charities, though I'm fairly hands off. My wife often gets more involved than me. We prefer to focus on small local charities where a smallish contribution can make a huge difference. And because of personal circumstances, we also focus on charities dealing with special needs' adults and children.

RC: **How many times did you submit to publishers before you had work accepted? Were you part of any fanzines back in the days of University?**

IR: We started a fanzine at Beath High. It was called *Mainlines*, which is a song by Doctors of Madness. At uni, I helped occasionally with the student newspaper and wrote film reviews for the Film Society bulletin. I did get a lot of rejection letters for my poems and short stories. My first novel, *Summer Rites*, is in the bottom drawer, having been turned down by everyone who saw it. My first Inspector Rebus novel was turned down by five or six publishers before finding a home. The moral being: never give up!

RC: **Now you're playing with the band Best Picture. Can you confirm that all writers want to be musicians and all musicians want to be writers?**

IR: That's actually truer than you might think but it's also a circle of sorts. Musicians want to be actors and actors want to be artists and artists want to be writers and writers want to be musicians . . . You can chop and change these but something like it is true. We all wish we were something else, but we've probably found the one thing we are good at and truly enjoy doing.

RC: **Tell us more about your book, *The Dark Remains*.**

IR: William McIlvanney was a writer I admired and he was a huge influence on my novels. At his death, he left behind some notes and scenes towards a crime novel set in Glasgow in 1972. His widow and publisher asked me to take a look, then asked me if I might consider finishing it. This was a huge honour but also a huge responsibility. I've done my best and everyone seems very happy with the result.

RC: **How instrumental is the role of your editor in terms of the quality of your finished pieces of work?**

IR: Not very, ha ha! That's going to piss off my editor. The thing is, I don't hand over any piece of work until I am 100% happy with it. My first reader is my wife and if she thinks a scene or character or piece of plotting doesn't work, I change it. So it has already been 'edited' before my agent and editor see it. The changes they ask for after that are usually cosmetic. I'll fight my corner if I think they want me to make a different book rather than a better book. There's that working class old punk thrawnness again!

LESBE FRIENDS
Fee Johnstone

Alice awoke in a crumple of itchy sheets and stale sweat in a bed she did not recognise. Her face was gnarled with dehydration, while her breath suggested a rogue feline had mistaken her mouth for a litter tray. Groggily, she sat up against the padded headboard as the remnants of her serene dreams faded into the reality of her surroundings: forlorn furniture, ripped netted-curtains and discarded cider cans.

As she surveyed the carnage of the room, she swallowed back the stomach acid that was migrating north. She tried to sit up but felt constrained – something was obstructing her breathing but, as panic ensnared her, she realised what was wrong: her internal organs were being compressed by the nanoscopic swimming costume in which she was clad.

What had happened? And where was she? All she knew was that she was festering in a bed that stunk of desperation, in an unfamiliar room, with an ill-fitting swimsuit wedged up her natal cleft.

There were no other signs of life in the room and what lay beyond the time-debased window provided no further clues: rows of graffitied tenements, a boarded-up corner shop and a rabid-looking man wearing a slipper for a hat, but nothing to explain the events leading up to her being garbed in beachwear from Mothercare. She examined the contents of her wallet, which were sprawled on the floor – her library card stared accusingly at her. It was then the memories of the previous 24 hours percolated into her consciousness like the saline drip to which she yearned to be attached.

Alice was 16 and had been struggling with her sexuality after realising she'd rather be Mariah Carey's 'Dreamlover' than Mark Owen's 'Babe', but she wasn't ready to tell the friends who still graffitied their school bags with 'Boyz Rule OK'. Therefore, she was feeling a little isolated but didn't know how to meet others like her. This was the early 90s when the only thing you used a computer for was saving Princess Peach whilst in the guise of a moustachioed plumber called Mario. The only real-life person she knew that likely played for Lemon FC was her masculine netball teacher whose moustache surpassed that of Mario's, and she wasn't about to swap girl crushes with her any time soon.

Not knowing what else to do, she'd gone to the library and stalked the Gender Studies section in the hope that some fellow gays would materialise, declare her wonderful and become her friend. But no-one came near as she sat cross-legged in front of the section, her eyes scanning the room as though she were a feral cat looking for sustenance. One day, just as she was considering life as a friendless nun, the neon pink cover of a book sat on a nearby chair beckoned her.

It was a book of gay classifieds, *The Pink Pages*, that listed all gay establishments in every British city. This was exactly what she was looking for! She excitedly flipped to her underpopulated hometown and found one entry: listed under the heading 'Guest House' was a place called The Red Bandana. The name was accompanied by nothing more than an address and a cute picture of two stick men. Alice had no idea what a gay guest house was, but she was going to find out. She ran home, crammed whatever clothes came to hand into a bag and offered her parents an excuse about staying at a friend's.

Using her dad's fold-out town map, she reached the address written on her forearm and knocked on the paint-cracked door, hands trembling. Her heart hammered, threatening to release itself from its prison of muscle and bone, but her face fell when a man wearing a leather vest opened the door. He was equally baffled to see Alice, but offered her a room regardless. She was ushered upstairs to a room decorated in all shades of vomit, but it was alright, she reminded herself, she was in a gay hotel!

She unpacked her scant belongings, realising in the hysteria of the moment that she had packed cans of cider, three socks and her favourite woolly jumper (despite it being summer), but no clean underwear or pyjamas. But wait, there was a swimsuit. How on earth had that gotten in? That godawful pastel pink thing her aunt had given her when she was ten years old. That was probably the last time her legs had been witnessed by eyes other than those of her cuddly toys.

After casting aside the offending article, she'd cracked open her first can of confidence. When she was four cans bolder, she'd peered into the dank hallway.

'Lesbehavingyou,' she called out hopefully, but the only reply forthcoming was that of some curious rhythmic thumps and odd wailings that appeared to be coming from downstairs. The owner must have cats, she deduced.

The hours had trickled by as steadily as the cider had trickled in and, aside from the bumps and caterwauling, all had been still. Unfortunately, the last memory Alice could elicit was defiantly resolving to wear her water-resistant leotard as pyjamas. The ensuing struggle to contort herself into the unforgiving Lycra incurred a bruised collarbone and an agonising wedgie, front and back.

But now, with some semblance of self-returning, Alice cringed as she wondered if she'd had the company she'd so desperately craved. The key in the inside of the lock told her that fermented apples had been her only accomplices and she sighed with relief (as best she could – she really must free herself from her suffocating attire). It didn't matter that she still didn't know what made a guest house gay, because there was plenty of time to familiarise herself with this new world. There would also be other opportunities to make gay friends – in more appropriate environments, and when her thighs were not ablaze with chafe.

And besides, she hadn't been entirely alone – around 10,000 bedbugs were attempting to occupy her orifices. Thankfully they were no match for snug spandex; apparently squeezing her bulk into Barbie's swimsuit had been a smart move after all.

SHOAP
Dickson Telfer

Ah walk intae a paper shoap. Behind the coonter is a young lassie, hair in pigtails, sookin a lollipop. As Ah approach, she puse it oot hur mooth, makin a pronounced POP! Ah kin smell synthetic strawberry.

'How may Ah help you, sir?' She strokes one o hur pigtails.

'Eh . . . 20 Lucky Strike, please.'

'Well, God damn, we have a fan of American tobacco in our midst,' she announces, cowgirl-esque. Kinda reminds me o Jessie fae *Toy Story 2*.

'They taste better,' Ah say, smilin.

She turns, lifts the flap an chucks the pack oan the coonter. 'Bit dae they make *you* taste better?' She pits the lollipop back in hur mooth an raises an eyebrow.

Ah look roond the shoap an take a breath. 'Depends. Dae ye like the taste o toasted tobacco?'

'Ah might dae. An Ah definitely like beards, especially ones like yours – ye ken, ones thit urr choaklit broon, bit wi a wee flicker o ginger an a wee flicker o grey.'

'Is that right?' Ah say.

'Yes it is, sir. Yes . . . it . . . is.' She rests hur foreairms oan the coonter, makin me look doon hur low cut top. Suckin loudly oan hur lollipop, she turns hur attention tae playin wi the bright-coloured beads oan hur wrist.'

Ah feel a sweat comin oan. 'How much dae Ah owe ye? Fur the fags?'

'Ye kin huv thum fur three quid if ye like,' she says, lookin up. 'Hey! Wur you lookin at ma tits?'

'Naw, naw, honestly Ah wisnae.' Ah hold out ma hands tae protest ma innocence.

She stands tall, scowlin, airms folded acroass hur chist. Ah shake ma hands, as if they're extra heids sayin naw naw.

'Why no?' Hur foreheid smoothens as hur airms droap by hur sides. 'Wid ye like tae touch thum? Ah mean, yer hands look like they're ready tae oanywey.'

'Whit?'

'Go oan.'

Ah fondle thum, egg-fryin heat oan ma face.

'Wait here,' she says, throwin oaff ma hands. Janglin keys, she skips tae the door, locks it, skips back an takes ma hand. 'Okay, come.' She leads me doon a corridor tae a door at the back o the shoap.

'Jist a minute,' Ah say, stoppin in ma tracks. 'Urr you legal?'

'Course Ah um!' she laughs, 'Ah work in a shoap thit sells fags n booze, don't Ah? Noo, come oan.'

She throws open the door tae the back room, an standin there, in fu uniform, baton in hand, is a polisman.

'Fuck *you* up tae?' he says.

LONDON'S CALLING
Saira Viola

Half-pint eyes trapped in emaciated light
children coddled tight,
Between ripped,
stinking bedsheets
and hatching lice –
feasting on the sweet, fresh blood
of their gold-top smiles

The hair of the night
cobwebbed with fear,
tattered tomorrows,
and a belly of tears

The open mouth
of the Gherkin city
spreads her famished grin
money talks boss –
but no-one's listening

SIX MILLION REASONS TO HATE
Quirk

It started with rhetoric and the painting of signs
On every shop window, being Jew was the crime
Then came the night of the breaking of glass
When the brown shirts wreaked havoc
Brought chaos and death . . .
More than six million reasons to hate

Like cattle they herded them into the ghettos
Dispossessed of their homes
Robbed of their shops
Left without anything, so cruelly starved
Abandoned, forgotten, made to wear stars . . .
More than six million reasons to hate

Taken from their ghettos under armed guard
Down to the stations and onto the tracks
Packed in tight on train after train
Destination unknown and never seen again . . .
More than six million reasons to hate

Forced into the showers when they disembarked
Possessions left scattered their card had been marked
From the heads of the showers rained Zyklon B to
Disinfect their bodies from lice and disease . . .
More than six million reasons to hate

Crammed tight into ovens their earthly remains
Men women and children slaughtered and slain
To leave our humanity indelibly stained
We must never forget it or it will happen again
The darkest of hours, the deepest of shame…
More than six million reasons to hate
More than six million reasons to hate

Razur Cuts interviews
JEAN-JACQUES BURNEL

Jean-Jacques Burnel (JJB) is a musician, producer and songwriter. He is best known as the bassist with The Stranglers, a band Razur Cuts has grown up with and followed since the early years, so this interview was extra special for us. We chatted with Jean-Jacques in January 2018.

RC: **How is life treating you, and how are things in The Stranglers camp?**

JJB: At the moment The Stranglers are in a good place. We've had a good few years of touring which has seen a noticeable increase in interest in the band, and now we are getting ready to record and are still writing.

RC: **The Stranglers are hardened tour specialists; how do you decide which songs to play? Also, how do you strike a balance between the must-plays and the tracks you want to play? Is there a song on the set list you'd consider dropping for a while?**

JJB: There are songs each member of the band prefers playing and some that we collectively get tired of, in which case we drop them until such time as we regain enthusiasm for them. If any member of the band objects to playing a song, we don't play it.

RC: **Has your approach to song writing changed over the years?** *Giants* **had a different feel and sound – was this you exploring a softer side?**

JJB: I'm not really aware of any change in our approach to song writing, although it must surely be a reflection of us at that moment in time. There would be no point in us trying to inhabit something we no longer are.

RC: **Do you think your views expressed on your solo album** *Euroman Cometh* **have come to fruition? Are there any plans for another solo album?**

JJB: *Euroman Cometh* reflects an idyllic version of how I envisaged how Europe should be. As far as solo work goes, the answer is no, all my energy is on The Stranglers.

RC: **Which Stranglers album is your favourite, or are they all so unique that it's difficult to choose?**

JJB: That's a very cruel question because each album represents a period in time and reflects what we were living through then. So, I have fonder memories of some than others. Musically, some are more coherent than others and some were more technically challenging than others. We always consciously tried to make each album different from the previous one, but that's probably not for me to say, being too close to them.

RC: **The Stranglers weren't recognised or named as being influences to younger bands, despite a Stranglers sound coming through. This now seems to be changing and we're happy about that. Are you aware of this?**

JJB: For a long period, other bands and musicians were scared to cite us as influences, although that was our generation of bands, because they didn't want to be associated with us for whatever reason. It annoyed me a bit, because we weren't manufactured and we took the brunt of hostility to whatever people perceived as being punk or new wave since we were out there in bum-fuck-nowhere and not just posing on the front cover of NME from an apartment in West London. Fortunately, that has changed.

RC: **Sadly, Holger Czukay, bass player of Can, passed away. You were a big fan of the band. Were they an influence on you from an early age and did you ever have the pleasure of meeting him?**

JJB: I was a fan of Can and other krautrock. I did indeed meet Holger Czukay in the offices of our A&R boss, Andrew Lauder, at United Artists, to whom they were signed. I also met with Michael Karoli and went to his house to check out his studio a few miles north of Nice in France.

RC: **It has always been well documented about your martial arts and the high level you have reached. Is this, and the joy of teaching it to others, still a big part of your life?**

JJB: I love karate and martial arts in general. It has helped me remain relatively grounded, but also helped maintain a level of physicality which, as we get older, starts diminishing. I love teaching my students and seeing them fulfil their potential, it's extremely rewarding. My only regret is that I don't always have time to dedicate myself 100 per cent to it.

RC: **The Stranglers are adored here in Scotland and you have legions of fans. We know you recognise and value this. Do you have any special memories of touring up here over the years?**

JJB: Our relationship with Scotland goes way back. Scots girls, Scots mates, Scottish police cells, whisky, Cullen Skink and Arbroath smokies!

DEBT
Mr Mo

I get woken by the debt that's barking at the bottom of the stairs, waiting to be fed.

I tiptoe slowly out of the bedroom so I don't wake the debt that's lying snoring in my bed.

I turn on the kettle fuelled by debt sitting next to the increasing pile of bills, which I haven't paid yet or even intend to.

After my coffee I have a shower and a shave and I walk the debts before driving my new debt to work.

When I get home from work, my debt meets me at the front door after another hard day.

My debt kisses me and asks me what I'd like for dinner while watching my favourite show on TV.

After dinner, my debt asks me where I'd like to go on debt this year. She's heard that the south of debt is lovely at this time of year.

And then she asks me if her debt looks nice – she only just got it done today – and if her debt looks big in the new debt she bought in the sales.

And then I think how sad I'd be if I didn't have all these debts.

It's the debts that keep me going, that get me up in the morning. I suppose that's why I go to work and why I haven't left them yet.

It's the debt that makes me happy, that puts the sunshine into my days.

I could be the poorest man on earth but I'm a millionaire as long as I've got my debts.

WHY BOTHER IN THIS LIFE?
Ella

why bother in this life
with things you could be doing
in a parallel universe

why waste your time
worrying about
what could have been

the other you
version 2.0
living the good life

in the best
of all possible worlds
be happy for them

they'd be sympathetic
if they knew you existed
through the wormhole

the one who never
listened to morrissey
never wrote poetry

no broken hearts
no breakdowns
no drama

no strawberry cremes
in their box of chocolates
they go running for fun

jesus christ
they sound awful
thank your lucky stars

BURNT ORANGE PEEL
Julie Rea

He drifted.

The tide came in and he drifted; floating on a neon pink Li-Lo, hand trailing in the water like a bone pickled in a jar. The rip current was strong, carrying him half a mile out. From the shore, he was a rose petal bobbing on the surface of an overflowing bath tub. Herring gulls circled across the empty sky. His belly sagged over the waistband of his blue shorts. The skin on his feet looked like burnt orange peel.

She hovered on the edge of the lounger. Restless, she stood up, tortoiseshell sunglasses entwined in her black hair. She'd noticed them looking, of course, the teenage boys, and had enjoyed slowly rubbing the lotion over her thighs. Creamy skin under spaghetti straps; a bead of sweat trickling down the length of her tanned stomach. She looked older than 14. Her little sister was dropping shells and conches into a red bucket. She sat cross-legged on a striped blanket, ponytail like a parched brown tongue. 'Hey,' she said, scraping a plastic spade over and over in the sand to make a narrow furrow. 'Where's Dad?'

The lifeboat crew used a scramble net. Cubes of white vomit clung to his chest like tiny meteorites. They knelt beside him, taking turns to place the heel of their hand on his breastbone, pushing down, then releasing; pushing, releasing. A tattoo of a bluebird on his shoulder, *Ellie* and *Libby* in faded smoke-coloured ink underneath. The main crew member, Earl – red-faced and wheezing – interlocked his fingers one last time, pressing hard; a spasm in his wrist. Herring gulls circled wearily. Earl's knees clicked as he stood up. The foamy spray sloshed onto the deck with a loud, dull whoosh. The body a slab of pink, with hairy toes.

SELECT A DIFFERENT RELIGION
Meek

You're breeding distemper, this disenfranchised
Faith
Waiting there you seem agitated
Your bones without flesh
Your body language unaltered

All of your parables in one crystal glass, held to
Your lips
As if you've recently been seduced by unholy Alliance,
my role; the marble
Ghost
It's true I am a father but I am no son

A whole host of big name casualties, parodies
Of themselves
Gravity sucks, didn't you know
I saw it scrawled on a road by some half-wit
With a sense of humour
And then I saw transparency in you

All my provisions gone, spent until replenished
In fits and bursts
Buffers only prolonging last rites
Confetti husks in a room violated, this hour
Extends, lengthens
Biblical terms.

Andrew Gardner

Greig Adams

Debs Mullen

Hendo

THE REAL HOUSEWIVES OF TAMFOURHILL
Scott T. Steel

Georgina Watson opened the cutlery drawer and took out a Philips screwdriver. Strange to have such a tool there but there was a purpose for it. She knelt on one knee, gently removed the screws and prised up the floorboard. She reached underneath and picked out the tub of cannabis resin, which was carefully placed against a joist.

Just the usual amount, she said to herself as she mixed it with the flour, sugar, butter, milk, raisins and dried mango, the special ingredients to her legendary space cakes.

Georgina had run the homely cafe in Tamfourhill since her husband had died 15 years previously. She had named it The Coughy Café – a tribute of sorts as he had died from acute bronchitis. Through years of experimenting and tweaking, her space cakes were now the sought after cuisine of thrill seekers who came from near and far to purchase the delicacies.

Georgina was ultra-careful to cover her tracks and the one time she inadvertently gave one of the cakes to Roberta McKell, she had to close early as Roberta had gone into fits of giggles before vomiting on the hand-knitted tea cosy. Luckily, it wasn't too busy that day so the flowery curtains were drawn as Roberta stared at the wall, mumbling to herself. Georgina helped her to her taxi and paid her fare.

'Mixing her medication again,' she said to the driver as she breathed a sigh of relief.

Business had been good from then on. Georgina chuckled to herself as she envisaged winning *The Great British Bake Off*, with Prue Leith scoffing her cakes and taking a whitey live on TV.

Denise Devlin was a pillar of society. A former councillor, she had served as Chairwoman of the Rotary Club, secretary of the Bowling Club and had run the local Girl Guides for many years. Awards adorned her living room wall and photographs with dignitaries had pride of place in her well-polished cabinet.

Always looking in pristine condition, she shopped at M&S, had a top of the range Audi in the drive and dined at top restaurants. All this from her income from a picturesque Bed & Breakfast. A cottage like something from a postcard, hanging baskets, neatly trimmed lawn and brightly painted window frames.

But why a B&B in Tamfourhill? It was hardly the place for such a dwelling. The only tourists in this neck of the woods were the darts team from the Plean Tavern through for a league game. This didn't seem to affect business and no-one seemed to question it as Denise was a likeable local celeb who did lots for the community.

The cottage held a secret though. Always busy with female clientele, Denise had amassed a myriad of contacts in the prostitution game. A nice wee quiet suburban house with bedrooms rented out at premium rates to the high class hookers who travelled from Scotland's main cities. Discreet and isolated, the setup was perfect and had been for years. So were the spoils that came with it.

A mother of seven sons, life had been a toil for Alison Donaldson. Her husband had buggered off once the going had got tough so she had to bring the boys up herself. It had been hard at times, working for a pittance, doing the housework, making ends meet and keeping the boys in line.

The boys had grown into men. Big strong men with a fearsome reputation, partly due to their amateur boxing days when some had won titles. Alison commanded their respect and was, despite her frail appearance, Head of The Family. She could be seen most days ambling from shop to shop around the area and stopping for a cup of tea at various houses for a friendly chat.

The protection money kept rolling in. Add this to the cash from the bouncers' agency she'd set up with the boys at the helm and things were looking good. People feared the Donaldsons. If you stepped out of line, or didn't pay your dues, one word from Mamma Donaldson and you were mincemeat. The boys even joked they were in a boyband called Take That . . . Ya Cunt.

Pauline Mathers looked like a poor soul. Unkempt and scruffy with dirty fingernails, people pitied her as she trundled past in her wheelchair, which itself had seen better days. Her hair was matted and one of the lenses in her glasses was cracked like a teenager's mobile phone screen. She was well known around the town, wearing a well-worn path, in and out the same shops and cafes.

People like routine and familiarity, it's a sense of contentment. It was for Pauline, as she followed the same schedule every day. Taxi to the toon centre, a few hours of the same circuit there, then taxi back for a buzz around the village before heading home.

She liked being back at home because this is where the real work began, which really excited her. The wig came off, the glasses ditched. She folded the wheelchair, walked over to the computer and laid down the eight credit cards she had acquired that day.

The wheelchair was the perfect height for reaching into bags and pockets. Honed over the years, her skills were second to none. She should be on stage for sleight of hand tricks, better than Jerry Sadowitz in her eyes. A wizard on the computer and an in-depth knowledge of how to clone credit cards, she got a thrill from mastering the new techniques that allowed her to stay one step ahead of the so-called experts.

The 28th of December was the date in the diary the ladies all looked forward to and yearned for. The build-up was more exciting than Christmas. They were there at 7pm prompt for the annual get together. The same table in The Hurlet that they always sat at, just to the left of the bar where they had a full view of the karaoke singers. The four bottles of Babycham were lined up as a guy with a bad stutter sang, 'Words Don't Come Easy'.

Pauline, the bookkeeper for the four, gently laid the envelope on the table as the ageing friends looked at it with excitement and trepidation. She asked who would like to open it, and Alison gladly obliged. It was the time they'd all been waiting for: who would be queen bee for earning the most cash that year?

There was a quick, high-pitched shrill from Denise as her name was read out. Congratulations were exchanged from the others as Pauline passed the small trophy to her under the table. The prestige and pride of having this on her mantelpiece meant more than any of her other possessions. The strong but competitive bond between the primary school friends had gone on for decades.

The after presentation party was back at Denise's cottage. The four of them were enthralled by the male strippers, galvanised by the space cakes and Dom Perignon. It was truly a night to remember. The Real Housewives of Tamfourhill in all their splendour. They would reminisce about this night on their month long Caribbean cruise later in the year.

A CULTURAL GUIDE TO CARLISLE #1: THE BIN OUTSIDE THE TRAIN STATION

Josh Holton

The bin is a squat, black cultural hub; a museum of Carlisle's consumption with exhibits that will be preserved in the gullets of gulls and the craws of crows.

Exhibit 1. Chewing gum that bided its time collecting agitated tooth prints and offering no nourishment in return. Pieces are displayed on top of the bin like barnacles.

Exhibit 2. Newspaper wrapped around greasy chips; local stories worn thin and transparent.

Exhibit 3. Chicken bones sucked meatless by slugs: a runic message legible only to the Pagans buried far below the city.

Exhibit 4. A Kopparberg bottle, its label peeling. Is it half empty of cider, or half full of piss? The riddle cannot be solved by smell.

Exhibit 5. A puddle, at the bin's base, digests green pennies, detaching them from wishes as they settle amongst the bitterest ends of fag butts.

These are the remnants of Carlisle's sons and daughters, who waited here to be transported somewhere else, the city having fed upon them heartily.

The bin also accepts submissions from those who remain and those who return home. One may jostle past big, inflated lads with arched backs and arms, swollen into right-angles beneath straining t-shirts, to make one's own contribution. Mine was the original hand scrawl of this text, torn from my notebook.

FITTING IN
Jared A. Carnie

I've no idea
what the fuck
you're meant to do
in Starbucks
or Nando's
or Subway

but they've all
been here so long
and everyone is
so used to them
it'd be like admitting
I don't know
how trousers work
or which bit's the road
and which bit's the pavement

so I just listen out
for the person in front
and ask for
whatever they're having
and pray to God
it's not something
I'm allergic to.

MOURNING POTION
Alice Rose

For the relief of grief – to be taken once daily.

1 tsp of lemon juice
1 tsp of chamomile tea
2 dock leaves
4 drops of their favourite nail polish
½ a cotton pillowcase soaked in tears
A Facebook message from someone you haven't spoken to in over a year, offering their condolences
A tooth from their best grin
The last page of their favourite book
A handful of freshly cut grass
A seashell or pebble from the last beach you visited together
6 shots of your favourite cordial
6 shots of your favourite spirit

To combine, place all ingredients in a mortar and pestle, hum a lullaby, then transfer to a Boston Shaker. Shake well.

For best results, pair with 731 hours of binged television.

Razur Cuts interviews
BIG JOHN DUNCAN

Big John Duncan (JD) is a Scottish musician who's been in many bands during his career, his most prominent being Washington grunge/alternative rockers Nirvana. John kindly gave us an interview before he took to the stage with Goodbye Mr McKenzie at Edinburgh's Liquid Rooms in December 2019.

RC: **Tell us a bit about yourself . . .**

JD: I was brought up in Muirhead, outside Glasgow, and attended Chryston Primary School, before moving onto Clifton High and Coatbridge High Schools.

I worked as a printer in my formative years and got into Glasgow School of Art, but I didn't like it at all – in fact, I hated it. I felt like an outsider when I was there. They were teaching things I had no interest in, so I quickly returned to my printing job.

RC: **Music at school – what are your memories? And what was your first favourite radio station?**

JD: I hated music at school, absolutely hated it, just like Art School! It was 'The Grand Old Duke of York' with some old granny playing piano and the class singing along. Music at school was non-existent.

The first radio station I listened to was Radio Caroline, which played old blues music. One of my older sisters said it was terrible, so that inspired me to listen to it more!

At home, my parents played traditional Scottish stuff and when my sisters eventually came home with all the 60s albums, like The Rolling Stones, Frank Ifield and The Kinks, I really started to get into music in a big way.

The bands and artists I loved listening to growing up were Johnny Winter, Rory Gallagher, Status Quo, T. Rex, Mud, Alice Cooper and The Sensational Alex Harvey Band.

When I got my first guitar, my hero was Noddy Holder of Slade. There was a photograph of him in *Sounds* magazine holding a bar chord and I worked out from the pic what he was playing, so I was able to do it myself.

My sister took me to see Slade at Greens Playhouse, Glasgow. The support that evening was The Sensational Alex Harvey Band. I was young and completely shitting myself as these guys were crazy. It was a fantastic experience for a young lad and I'm still a big fan of the band.

RC: **Tell us about your invitation to join The Exploited**

JD: I played in a few bands and left my printing job to work in Listen Records in Glasgow. I realised the printing job was basically financing my musical career. My amps and guitars were all bought from the money I made at the printing company, but I had to enhance my musical career, so working in Listen helped me as they were more lenient with time off and flexible with my hours. We had a massive array of records and T-shirts. Downstairs, you could buy black and white pics from the latest Apollo gigs, just days after the event. What a great record shop.

RC: **We remember you working in Listen Records. You were wearing a *Dennis the Menace* jumper and had with orange hair!**

JD: Ha ha, you name a colour and I've had my hair that colour at least three times!

The guy at Listen opened a shop in Edinburgh and asked me to help set it up, which I was delighted to do. We played punk songs all afternoon on a Saturday, so the shop was always busy with punks browsing records. Everyone was friendly and I'd get invited to different bands' rehearsals on a Saturday evening, one of which was The Exploited.

One evening, when I'd gone along to one of their rehearsals at a venue in Niddrie Street, their bass player didn't turn up, so I stood in. Then, during a break, I picked up the guitar and played a few pieces, some Be-Bop Deluxe and Sensational Alex Harvey Band. Heads turned as people realised I could play a bit! A week later they sacked their guitarist and gave me the job.

RC: **You always said your most creative period was with The Blood Uncles. Can you elaborate on this for us?**

JD: Yes, to this day it's still the same. Everything we did was homemade – the music, the photography, the recordings and the record sleeves – all DIY. There was a concept behind that original EP, *Petrol*. We also recorded 'Let's Go Crazy' by Prince, which we absolutely loved and put on the album *Libertine*. We were told Prince had heard our version, which was nice to learn, but there wasn't much in the way of feedback.

RC: **Then there was The Gin Goblins. We saw you in Cumbernauld one Sunday evening.**

JD: Ah, I remember the venue in Cumbernauld, high up near a car park. Our lead singer's girlfriend, Jess, worked in a props department and would appear with all this amazing stuff for us to use, which we took full advantage of. The Gin Goblins line-up was: Mikey Jacobs on lead vocals, The Rev Dave Martin on guitar, Coco J Whitson on bass, Wullie Buchan on drums and me on lead guitar. Wullie went back to join The Exploited and was subsequently replaced by Chris Logan, who took over the drum stool for the *Season of The Dead* EP.

RC: **Then you joined Goodbye Mr McKenzie. You've had an amazing musical career, John.**

JD: Ha ha, yes, I've been around! I was in a club, tripping away, chatting to this guy who happened to be Martin Metcalfe. I didn't know who he was at the time, but we chatted about music for ages. He told me his band, Goodbye Mr McKenzie, were about to start recording and I was invited along as he knew I was a guitarist. I don't know why he asked me, because Martin is an excellent guitarist himself.

So, I did a session with them and it went really well – I was then invited to do a gig at Queen Margaret Union in Glasgow and it progressed from there. The first Goodbye Mr McKenzie album was recorded in Munich at Music Land where Queen recorded all their early material. The second album was recorded in Berlin at Hansa Tonstudio, where David Bowie, Iggy Pop and U2 had previously recorded.

RC: **That second album was in 1989. Were you aware of what was happening as you recorded, in regard to the wall coming down?**

JD: We were completely unaware of what was happening. We were in the studio one day and this guy came in shouting, "They're taking the wall down!" Looking back, it was a very surreal moment.

RC: **What happened when you left Goodbye Mr McKenzie and moved on to other things?**

JD: Rona Scobie had already left, so Martin and I got together with Shirley Manson and rehearsed as Angelfish. The songs were much lighter, songs that were left over from previous Goodbye Mr McKenzie material. At the same time as Angelfish, I got a phone call from a friend, Ali, saying he was working with a band called Nirvana, who were looking for a guitar technician – so I jumped at the chance!

RC: **When you tied in with Nirvana, was it before they became massive?**

JD: It was around the turning point as *Nevermind* had just been released. I got the guitar technician job off the back of being friends with Ali, who was originally the van driver for The Cateran, a band Nirvana supported at a gig in Edinburgh. The bands hit it off and, as a result, Ali ended up becoming Nirvana's tour manager, driving them to gigs around Europe as their popularity increased.

There was a great Scottish contingency with Nirvana actually; Derek Kelly of Goodbye Mr McKenzie ended up looking after the drums for Dave Grohl, and Ian Beveridge was their monitor engineer.

RC: **Kurt Cobain was into wonderful Scottish bands, like The Vaselines and Teenage Fanclub. He always struck us as a shy retiring type of guy who was just into his music. Was this the case?**

JD: Kurt was very much into his music and he and the band could handle the fame, but I feel they were forced into positions they didn't want to be in. People wanted Kurt to be at the centre of the stage and he wouldn't do it. At the famous live MTV show, *Nirvana Unplugged*, the cameras, lighting and amps were all set up for Kurt to be in the middle, but he point-blank refused, so everything had to be reorganised, which took hours. He sits at the end of the stage for the whole set. Looking back at my time with Nirvana, I wish I'd taken more pictures!

RC: **Who's the most interesting person you've met?**

JD: Very good question. I'd say meeting Bill Nelson was a tremendous experience. It was after a gig at Edinburgh Playhouse. We sat and spoke about guitars and the time flew by. I was a massive fan of Bill and Be-Bop Deluxe. A fantastic memory to hold.

RC: **How is life in Amsterdam where you live now?**

JD: It's wonderful. I'm so glad I'm there and not here!

RC: **How were you contacted about the Goodbye Mr McKenzie reunion?**

JD: We all stay in touch regularly and I was asked about the reunion gigs. I didn't think I'd be able to take part as I now have MS. At home in Amsterdam, I revisited the albums by playing along on bass. I realised I could still play, and with encouragement from my partner I picked up my guitar and, before I knew it, I was confident enough to be able to make a decision to play the reunion.

There was a build up to me finding out I had MS. I was walking to work one day and I had developed a limp, but with no pain. My neck and arm had also gone numb. I had convinced myself I'd had a stroke. So, I had all the tests and an MRI scan. After these tests, they diagnosed me as having MS.

The nurse at the hospital told me in no uncertain terms not to look up MS on the internet, so guess the first thing I did once I got home? I read everything I could on the subject and took all the medical advice I was given. It's exceptionally unusual for a male over 55 to contract MS and I was exactly 55 when I was diagnosed.

Since I've returned to music, I've stopped my medication, a drug called Aminex I had to inject into both my legs once a week. I take no injections now; the power of music has given me a new lease of life. When I'm up on stage, it feels like it's where I belong; that's my new medication.

We played Dingwalls in London and I managed to walk from the hotel to the venue, play the gig, meet people afterwards for a chat, then walk back to the hotel. That was an amazing feeling and the best therapy I could ever have asked for. I felt tremendous, so tremendous that I wanted to throw my crutches away!

RC: **The initial punk and new wave ethos was DIY in all forms. Did you embrace this attitude?**

JD: Yes, very much so. I loved the "just get up and do it" free-for-all, the power of the heart and mind. Music has become big business again though. These talent shows on TV when people sit and hit a button is utter shite to me. Kids are aspiring to this garbage. Dave Grohl has a great theory about it – get together with your mates and just do it to make yourself feel good. And fuck off if you don't like it!

RC: **Were you comfortable with the Mohican style punk thing as opposed to the original punk and new wave scene?**

JD: I'm glad you asked that. Not many people know that that style came from somewhere else. If I see someone dressed like that nowadays, I tell them straight, 'You're not a punk!' For fuck's sake, Madonna is more of a punk, she has attitude!

Punk, for me, questioned fashion through people creating their own clothing, DIY-style. The original scene was about change – in music and clothing – and moving forward with both.

RC: **Then we had post-punk. What were your thoughts on that progression?**

JD: I thought the bands were great. Joy Division and Killing Joke were exceptional. Even bands like The Clash and The Buzzcocks evolved over time.

The only music I couldn't get into was reggae. I found it difficult to connect for some reason. My friends and I would go to a reggae club to get a late drink and a smoke. They would be up skanking away, but I didn't join in at all. I've noticed throughout the years that if I don't like a certain genre, I grow to detest it! Then again, I could listen to some Yellow Man and Black Uhuru. Bob Marley took reggae and made it his own by moulding it to suit his unique style.

RC: **Tell us something we don't know about you?**

JD: That's easy, I'm a dab hand with a sewing machine. Everywhere I've lived, I've owned and regularly used one. It's a passion of mine. I fix and make clothes. Brilliant fun!

RC: **Do you do anything musically in Amsterdam?**

JD: I work in a venue as the sound engineer and have jam sessions with my friends, Fiona and Roger. We've actually recorded material but nothing has been released to date.

THE KEYCHAIN
Rob Plath

When I was 12 years old
I found a keychain
in my father's drawer

A mould of a naked couple
Standing facing one another
Hinged by a rivet

I swivelled it back and forth
And the man's large erection
Seemed to disappear

Between the thighs of the woman
With the large breasts

And I wanted to snap
That ugly couple in half
But instead I placed it back beside
The knives and the pistol

Helen McGinn

stonedart

Colin Dalglish

Andrew Gardner

REMEMBRANCE SUNDAY
Ian Parris

A pensioner approaches the cenotaph, lays a wreath, back-pedals and salutes. It was the last wreath and it's now the start of the two-minute silence signalled by a rifleman firing into the air.

Everybody looks at the ground, at the birds in the sky, thoughts a million miles away. There are young soldiers who must be back from a tour of duty in Iraq, Afghanistan or Libya. We're fighting in so many places it's easy to lose track. Some dusty, desert outpost anyway. They'll probably have to return to the front line afterwards. Probably know of someone who has died recently. Someone who's given their life for king and country. And I wonder if the soldiers over there wonder whether it's all worth it, although I don't suppose they have the time at this stage. That always comes later. But I'm only going off the films and books. How they always portray the veteran as a sociopath. He's seen the lies at the heart of society.

There's a few old bods in uniform and I don't know where they got them from because my grandad was in the army, and although he's got his medals on, he doesn't have a uniform in his wardrobe. Today he's just got on his big coat that he's had for as far back as I can remember.

It's grey, overcast and bitter cold. My head's fuzzy as well cause last night I was on the *Dirty Harry* Colt 45 lager. It blows your head clean off. I'm still smelling of it and I've got the slow brain to match. The cars have been stopped, and they're waiting to go again but no-one's going to start peeping their horns at a remembrance day ceremony. The two-minute silence is dragging on. Another bloke over the other side is wearing medals but he's too young to have fought in the Second World War and he's too old to have fought in Afghanistan and so I wonder whether he fought in the Falklands war. I'm too young to remember it but it seemed a realer war. The Falklands are green, cold and windy, just like it is in this country, compared to these recent wars that are usually fought in hot dusty places.

Maybe it was cause as a country we were fighting alone then. Or because it was a shorter war, it was more intense and a bit more nerve-racking. Many were killed in a single day when one of our battleships was sunk. It was the opposite of these modern day conflicts where the fatalities are drip-drip-drip so people become immune to it. The footage of soldiers in green camouflage and boot polish on their faces and looking scared; maybe the Falklands seemed more real because those soldiers looked wary and vulnerable. I also associate soldiers in modern wars with those two princes and so you start to assume it's a bunch of toffs out there. You don't mind so much if they get their heads blown off. But suddenly I remember reading the Falklands was the first war where it was televised live. The scenes being beamed back home as they happened. Everybody crowded around their TV sets. The first of their magnificent peepshows.

The two-minute silence ends with another shot from the rifleman's gun, and then another, and I wonder if they're trying to shit the old boys up. I put an arm around my grandad and steer him gently in the right direction as we set off on the walk up the steep hill. It'll take 20 minutes to get home and he needs a stick, but hopefully he'll feel better for coming out this morning. I could have brought the car down, but the exercise and fresh air will do him good. Tire him out so he'll appreciate the rest when he has chance.

We arrive at the house and I stay and have a brew with him and I ask him what's on the menu for dinner cause he's big on his meals, although sometimes you think it's just something for him to do. He says he's not hungry yet but he's got a curry to put in the microwave. He likes his curries. He was in Egypt during the war but that's not where he got the taste for them from. In fact, he says they weren't allowed to eat the food in those hot foreign places because of the diseases they could pick up. They would be punished severely if they were caught in local restaurants.

I mention the Spurs-Everton game being on later and he says he'll probably watch it, although he doesn't sound too interested even though I know he's keen on his sport. You can still have a good discussion with him. He's not like a lot of old bods who've given up on the sport. Mention football and they go into one about how the players these days are all scumbags. Wear earrings, and wear gloves in September. They're bringing the game into disrepute. Calling the players all the names under the sun. Lots of old blokes have given up on football. And maybe 30 or 40 years of following the beautiful game is enough for most. But hopefully I'll be like the old man who doesn't approach football with the usual old man's take on things. Has a brain of his own and can decide for himself about how things have changed. He's told me before that the girls used to throw themselves at the footballers-of-old, waiting for them outside the ground after the match and promising them things, promising them everything, no shame. Yet the way you hear some old fellas talk, you'd think footballers in the old days used to be celibate. Spent their Friday and Saturday nights doing charity work.

I have to tell my grandad that I need to leave. That I'm meeting up with my friends and I ask if he wants to come, knowing the old boy will refuse. He's had his day out today and now just wants to relax and it was good to be able to help him. My grandma passed away a few months ago and so he's still struggling to cope with the loss. It's the reason for the photo frame propped up on the kitchen table. A bit freaky. But it can't be easy when you've lived with someone for 60 years and you did everything together. I suppose it's why I took him to the service. Making an effort with him. Makes me feel closer to my grandma as well if I'm honest. She only went into hospital with a broken wrist but she got that MRSA disease, where the hospitals are dirty, and then suddenly there were complications. She started going downhill rapidly. I suppose a person could get angry but she died youngish for an old woman and wasn't somebody who had to fight cancer for years, nor did she have to go through the indignity of going in a home, something she would've hated – so that's something Not that the hospital knew any of this when they were doing a bad job of treating her.

I'd worn a shirt, tie and a long coat to the cenotaph but it's a bit too formal for the pub. I get back home, eat a quick sandwich, get changed and head straight back out the door. I walk to the pub with a pocketful of change, without a single note, but I should be grateful for the coins because once they're gone, I'll be skint. Today I won't spend a fortune. And last night had been a cheap one, just a few cans round at Dave's. Six cans of strong lager putting me in a happy state. When Dave sorted out some music, it was the nail in the coffin for going out. A bit of an unsociable way to spend Saturday night but Dave said he needed to save money too. Said it was something he might have to consider doing more of in the future, cause of the price of beer in the pubs. I didn't mind stopping in on Saturday night but it's only cause I knew I was coming out today. You need the interaction that you get down the pub. This afternoon, I'll just have five or six pints. Give me a bit of a social life. Don't feel like I have an alternative really.

The town's never really recovered from the decline of the old industries. The disappearance of the factories and engineering works and mills and mines. Leaving behind huge derelict buildings, ten storeys high. Or one storey factories that cover the size of a couple of football pitches and now just the factory floor remains, like where a tooth's been yanked out of its socket. It's not just the tooth that's gone but the roots. And a well-paid factory job can keep a lot of kids fed and houses maintained and local shops going. They've been knocking the mills and factories down for decades and there's still quite a lot left showing how many there once were. Fuck all of anything of that size that employs people in this town these days. Jobs on the council but even it's making cutbacks. The big supermarket chains would pat themselves on the back but the only employment they provide is part time and minimum wage. Supermarkets provide fuck all of a lifeline. Driving local shopkeepers out of business more like. Companies that'll crush anything that gets in their way with their hired experts and lawyers.

Maybe being on the dole's affecting my mood, making me negative, but I'm cheering up as I arrive at the pub, going up the steps and through the door. I instantly see Don and Chris looking in my direction, but only because they're watching the big TV screen near the door, one of those screens that pulls down from the ceiling, a full-wall job, a few rows of people gazing at the screen like they're retarded. A few birds as well cause it's Sunday. Everyone putting off thoughts of work tomorrow. Or putting off thoughts of no work tomorrow.

'Alright, lads?'

'Yeh. You, Tom?'

'Yeh, I've just been to the cenotaph with my grandad. I just went home to change my coat. Get out of my big trench coat.'

'I didn't know you fought in the war, Tom?'

'Yeh, I look good for my age, don't I?'

Don and Chris haven't much beer left in their glasses and I ask what they're drinking, say I'll get the round in but they'll have to hurry up cause I don't want to miss the start of the match. Don nods at the screen. 'There's plenty of time. They're just doing the minute's silence. I bet you'll have done this today already, haven't you? You're going to spend half the day in silence. Thank fuck.'

It's busy at the bar but I manage to get the three pints in quickly. I get back and hand the drinks out and I look at the screen and the two sets of players and officials are all stood around the edge of the centre circle with their heads bowed. Pub chatter encroaches on the silence for a bit, but it soon dies down. Not a single comment. No belches or farts. The screen is showing pictures of fans and the wind's up and it's obvious because you can see it blowing people's hair around, girls' especially, and there's noises in the street from outside the ground, the world going on as normal. The silence is two minutes instead of the usual one but it's still being upheld. The referee blows the whistle and there's a big roar at the ground and the chatter starts up in the pub again like a switch has been flicked. The two minutes at the ground was well respected and they didn't even have to resort to a minute's applause. At the football, there were no trendy cunts in the crowd who would never buy a poppy because it condoned violence. Near perfect silence in the pub as well. The old boy would have been proud.

The screen shows a couple of fighter planes now. Darts roaring across the sky. And Don asks if we can remember the time that parachutist tried to land on the centre spot at Turf Moor. It'd been organised by the club but he ended up landing on the roof of the Cricket Field stand and the referee wouldn't start the game for about 15 minutes until he was rescued. That's typical Burnley. Couldn't arrange a piss-up in a brewery. A milkshake in a dairy. Then Don is saying the parachutist should've been booked for descent.

Spurs-Everton is underway and it's a decent game for the neutral. Two attacking teams and both will feel they can win the game. The Premiership at its best. Why more people watch this league than any other in the world. The action comes at three times the rate of action in an Italian goalless bore-draw. Of course at half-time it's nil-nil. The game stuttering like a shit-heap of a car. Stuttering like George VI. Don hands out the pints on his return from the bar and breaks some news. 'Have you heard Pete's got a new bird? He met her on the internet.'

'You should never shop online,' says Chris. 'The odds are good but the goods are odd.'

'There's dodgy birds in town too, there's dodgy birds everywhere, you might as well take your chances on the internet, especially if it means you're going to get a gobble at the end of it. The end justifies the means. Is she alright?'

'Yeh he was in here with her the other night. She's nice enough. Although she's from Blackburn. She's Rovers.'

'He's sleeping with the enemy.'

'Yeh, apparently they're even going on a city break next weekend,' Don continues. 'She had her heart set on Amsterdam but he managed to talk her into going to Paris instead.'

'It would've been a bit tricky going to the Dam. Worrying if any of the birds in the windows might recognise him as he's passing.'

Don goes to the bog and I ask Chris if he's still working in the demolition game.

'Aye, we're working down Burnley Wood at the moment. We pulled about ten streets down in a week. We've torn down loads of houses already, there's loads more waiting to be demolished and the other streets have half their houses boarded up. Yeh, we're knocking so many houses down, Burnley will soon be just a wilderness again. Lions and tigers roaming about.'

'That's how Sharpy's uncle made his money,' says Don coming back from the bog and joining in the conversation. 'Boarding houses up. He started out as a joiner and then he set up on his own. He got a big contract with the council. He must be a millionaire easy. I went to his house once. A big farmhouse at the end of a long farm track with an ornamental duck pond out the front. He keeps hens as well and they wander about all over the place. The taxi driver nearly ran a few over as, pissed up, we left.'

I take a sip of my pint and see the game's restarting. It's true about Burnley being on its knees; looks like Dresden after Bomber Harris had finished with it. Or like Portsmouth when the Luftwaffe had been over it to soften it up for the invasion that never materialised. That's the way our town looks now. They're pulling down all the mills and factories and terraced houses. The Germans shouldn't have bothered trying to invade when they did. They should've just waited. We've done it to ourselves. What the Germans didn't manage to do, it's been done anyway.

Razur Cuts interviews
TONY DRAYTON

Tony Drayton (TD) is the founder of one of the very first fanzines to materialise from the punk/new wave scene back in the mid to late 70s. His fanzine was called *Ripped & Torn*. It ran for 18 issues, all of which have recently been reproduced in book form. He kindly gave us an interview in April 2019 about his time as the editor of his now legendary fanzine.

RC: **What gave you the impetus to start your own fanzine and how did you go about the process ahead of your first release?**

TD: This punk rock phenomena was being written about in the music press by journalists I respected. I devoured those music papers on my daily commute to work from Cumbernauld to Glasgow and this punk stuff was really talking to me, making me feel *This is it! This is what I've spent all my life waiting for.* At that point I hadn't thought about being part of it, let alone writing a fanzine.

However, on a trip to London in November 1976, I saw The Damned play the Hope & Anchor – the first time I got to experience a punk gig – and things accelerated somewhat. This was better than I imagined, not just the music but the whole ambience of the event. I spoke to Mark P there, who was behind the *Sniffin Glue* fanzine, and asked if I could write for him about my experience of punk that evening. Mark said, "No, go back to Scotland, start your own fanzine and write about it in that". That was the impetus to start *Ripped & Torn*. I went back to Cumbernauld and within a week or so had put together the first issue, basing it on the *Sniffin Glue* template of ten A4 pages, one-sided printing and stapled in the corner.

That week consisted of my like-minded friend Phil and me writing eight pages of reviews, my memory of The Damned gig, plus a front cover and back page pin-up using pictures cut out of the music press. I made ten copies, stapled them up and that was the first release. As far as I was concerned, that was all it was going to be. I sent one to Mark P to show him I did it. I also sent copies to Rough Trade record shop and Compendium bookshop in London, and that changed everything.

RC: **Did you have new contributors each issue submitting material about bands you were possibly unaware of? Did you welcome anyone to be part of the fanzine or did you have criteria for submissions?**

TD: There was no policy regarding contributors. At the start it was just me and Phil, who published under the name Skid Kid. In the second issue, Sandy Robertson wrote some things and by the fourth issue there was a young contributor called Edwyn Collins who wrote about record shops in Glasgow.

Once in London, I started getting loads of photos sent to me by aspiring snappers, brilliant live pictures that I used. Some of these pictures were of bands I was unaware of at the time, so they helped me check them out. It was rare to get unsolicited writing though. What tended to happen was someone speaking to me at a gig and asking if I wanted them to write about something in particular.

One person who sent writing in was Jeremy Gluck from Canada. I printed his work as it was well written and about bands no-one in Britain had ever heard of. He eventually came over to London and became a regular writer, at the same time forming a band called The Barracudas who had a smash hit record with 'Summer Fun'. Excellent band. He also went on to write for *Sounds* music paper.

RC: **Once you had the material collated, at what point did you realise it was time for a new release? Did many bands send you their new singles and albums for reviewing?**

TD: It was more a case of when I'd sold out of an issue, I thought about creating a new one. Occasionally I attempted to have a structure and publishing deadlines, but as no-one but me cared, issues were just printed and sold as and when. I'd always be thinking about the next issue though, and at gigs would be considering interviewing bands or writing reviews when I got home – or a few days later if I didn't get home. An indication of this is issue 12, which has the date on it as simply 'Summer'.

Review copies: As I collected my mail from Rough Trade, the people there played me new releases on small labels and I reviewed them in the shop or bought them to review at more length later. As for the larger labels, I used to make regular visits to places like CBS, RCA, EMI and Warner Brothers' offices in order to get given review copies of new releases. Sometimes I would also be able to persuade the promotional people to give me stuff not obviously punk related, like David Essex, The Eagles or Demis Roussos, which was nice. Once I remember not having enough money to pay the printer, so I went round the record companies, got as many promotional records as I could and then sold them at Record & Tape Exchange, making enough to cover my printing costs. Good stuff, though I remember to this day the angst in having to sell a Bowie double live album I really wanted to keep.

RC: **Please tell us of how a massive DIY fanzine from Cumbernauld in Scotland managed to distribute to its readers back in the late 70s?**

TD: In Cumbernauld, I sent bulk amounts of issues to Rough Trade and Compendium, both in London, and presumed they distributed them. I sold them via independent record shops in Glasgow, on a sale or return basis. I moved to London in March 1977 and the Cumbernauld link ended from issue five onwards.

RC: **How much did you charge for each issue and did you have subscribers from afar?**

TD: The cover price was 25p. Subscriptions were a nightmare – people sending coins, foreign notes, postal orders, stamps and all sorts for individual issues. These came from all over the world, a lot from Scandinavia for some reason, but also many from America. I remember spending days with piles of envelopes deciphering names and addresses scribbled on bits of paper, trying to get issues posted out to everyone. In issue seven, I reviewed a couple of punk bootlegs, which led to me getting sent money to buy copies and post them out, which I did.

Standing in the post office trying to fathom the various overseas postal rates and parcel or package weights, I remember thinking *This isn't what I became a punk for!*

RC: **Who were your favourite bands of that time and, if possible, what was your favourite issue of *Ripped & Torn*? In total, how many issues were there?**

TD: There were 17 issues, plus a two-page *Ripping Christmas* edition, so 18 in all. A contributor called Vermilion Sands produced one issue after I went to Europe in the summer of 1979 but that was *Ripped & Torn* in name only.

My favourite issues are from issue ten onwards, February 1978 to March 1979. I really found my voice and style then. 1978 was a great time in London with loads of punks from all over the world descending on the place looking for action, at the same time the music industry and press were trying to kill it. *Ripped & Torn* stepped into the void and was really the voice of the people of the time – at one point we were the only place you could read about Adam and the Ants, and then Crass a little later.

I was the first person to interview Adam Ant, his interview appearing in issue eight. By issue 14, Adam and the Ants were massive and our interview was a sensation. It was the same with Crass. I was the first person to interview them and their interview was published in issue 16, with a live review and album review in issue 17. Both bands were missed or deliberately shunned by the music press. We also covered The Banshees extensively before they were belatedly signed. I slag off their debut as being several years too late.

Raped were another favourite band. They featured on the cover of issue 11, which caused problems! They never received the acclaim they deserved though, despite changing their name to Cuddly Toys.

RC: **You live in London. Do you still attend gigs regularly? Do you have any new bands you're into that you'd like to share with us? Do you feel you've evolved as a music fan by opening up to different genres, or do you still only listen to punk? Was post-punk as important to you? At Razur Cuts, we feel we've evolved – this has enabled us to be more understanding of different styles and the inspiration bands take from others as time moves on.**

TD: A friend turned me on to Jim of Carter USM's new band, Jim's Super Stereoworld. I followed them around until they split up. I loved them. Jim still does solo acoustic gigs with a mix of new,

Stereoworld and Carter songs, and occasionally I go to hear the Stereoworld ones. Linked to the Stereoworld crowd was a band called Art Brut, who supported them sometimes. I started following them around too, also loving them. Linked to Art Brut was a band called Video Club, and I started following them around and loving them as well.

All of that died off a bit for me about ten years ago and now I live in a musical bubble – listening to artists I already know, mainly via YouTube, but more obscure tracks and versions of songs. For example, I've been playing obscure Jimi Hendrix songs. What caused this die-off is having kids, basically!

As for evolving, I've always liked a wide range of music, even in the punk days, so it's not my range that's narrow, but I tend to only listen to music from a certain time. Art and other aesthetics have also entered my world over the years and given me enjoyment, architecture for example. I never knew I could get a thrill from looking at a building!

MORNING HAS BROKEN
Michael Keenaghan

Daylight. Staring into the bathroom mirror. Your eyes, look at them. The fear in them. And your hands, they're shaking; you're trembling all over. Stop this, right now, go back to bed. But you can't. You've got to work. Get to the office and work. Things to do, out there in the real world, away from all this. Got to remind yourself it's just a morning thing; the rush of fear, rush of panic. Everything magnified. All your mistakes, all the damage you've done. Your whole world ready to crash in, drill a hole through your brain, up against the wall, raped, mutilated, flayed alive, you're coming to hell you bastard.

No. Snap out of it. Turn away. And you do. Pissing into the toilet now. But look at yourself. The things you've done. You're evil, do you know that? But of course you do. Can feel it pulsing through your system like a curse. Every morning shivering, sweating, stinking of last night's drink. Go on, get it out, rid yourself of that poison. But you can't, can you. The sickness deep within, etched there like a rot, a deep putrid stink.

No wonder Carolyn left you in the lurch. Wife, two kids – then suddenly nothing. You in this family home all by yourself. Just you and the memories. Remember the time in the kitchen you grabbed her by the hair. Do you remember that? Really went for her that time, didn't you? Carolyn clutching her head where it had smacked against the edge of the cupboard. What a bastard. Gushing out apologies, swearing you were sorry, it would never happen again. But it did though, didn't it.

And look at yourself, brushing your teeth now, terrified of facing the light of day. Not surprising really. She's not coming back you know. I mean, you do know that, don't you? Forget what she said about thinking it over, those were just words. You're alone now. This is it. This is how it's going to be from now on. Carolyn, the kids – they hate you. Your own children – frightened of you. Feel pain, fear, every time they think of you. Your own kids.

Remember the football incident. No? Of course you fucking do. Comes out to bite pretty often that one doesn't it. Carolyn out shopping and you in with the kids watching the football. It was the Saturday after you'd lost out on the promotion, wasn't it. Day after the night before. Let him relax, go on, let Daddy sit and watch his football – delicate Daddy with his sensitive eyes, ears, his pounding head. But Amy, two, and Jack, four, running around making a right racket. Jack especially. Jack who you had told two, three, four times already. Head thumping with pain after having drunk yourself into a stupor, in the pub throwing back shorts long after your workmates had left, trying to initiate conversation with strangers and nobody interested, then staggering home and puking into the neighbour's front garden, and look at you now, the state of you, and the kids running and tearing, every sound cutting through your skull, and Jack Jesus Christ if I have to tell you again, and he kicks a toy that goes flying, the screams going right through you, and you grab him, shake him, roar your frustration into his face, then you push him and he goes flying, crashing into his toys.

He's looking at you, in shock, in fear, then he goes running crying out of the room, Amy following – Jack, I'm sorry – and Carolyn appearing at the door, dropping her bags and holding the children close to her, and you saying it was an accident, you were sorry, you never meant it, you . . .

You make me sick.

And look at you, shaving now, scraping that thing across your neck. Why don't you put that razor to some proper use, stop kidding yourself, living in a fucking fantasy. No-one's stopping you, you know. Think of it. Not going into work, not today, not ever, and the police coming round to break the door down. Or maybe Carolyn herself, suddenly wondering, suddenly caring, coming home to stay at last. And you there hanging from the ceiling with your wrists all slashed and a smile carved across your face, a sad happy clown, a dead fucking carcass, all you've ever deserved, everyone out of their misery.

But it's not going to happen, is it. Too much of a coward for that kind of thing, aren't you. In fact, you're too much of a coward for a lot of things. Take the other evening for example, coming out of the tube. Young bloke asks you for a cigarette, a teenager, and you give him one. Then next minute he's strutting next to you down the side street, asking for money, needs it to get home, what about a pound then, a fucking pound, what do you mean you haven't got it? Commenting on your suit and tie, telling you you're lying, look fucking loaded. But you insist, tell him you're skint, and he gives up, lets you walk on. Tutting at you. Goading you. Fuckin prick. I'll come round your yard and rob the place, ya fuckin pussy.

And what did you do, what did you even say? Nothing. Just walked. Heart beating. Kept moving. Bastard shouting at you. You, who had spent 12 hours sweating over that sale, sweating, fretting, stressed to the hilt, with your wife gone, your kids gone, your debts, your bills, your mortgage, knowing if this sale doesn't go through you might as well be dead – with some total stranger, some ignorant fool threatening you, goading you on the street?

Why didn't you do something? Turn round and charge him, knock him into next week. You could have you know. In truth, he was nothing but a mouthy little runt. You could have done anything, gone fucking wild, left him battered and bruised. Go round insulting strangers and you're taking a big risk. Don't these people realise that?

Maybe they do. And that's when he would've pulled his knife out, plunged it in without a care. You there fighting with your fists and him stabbing away like nobody's business. Alone on the street, clutching your stomach, blood running through your fingers. Man stabbed. Killed. It's all you ever hear about.

But why would you care? What have you got to protect now anyway? It's all gone. Disappeared. But you don't want to hear that, do you? Of course you don't. You'd run a mile rather than hear the truth. Run to the ends of the earth. Head in the sand. A beach somewhere. Black, polluted. Body dead. Writhing with maggots. For fuck's sake. You splash your face with water. Go on, get out of here.

Coffee. Now. You head to the kitchen in your boxers, watching the kettle as it heats. Body exhausted, mind alive. Flashing back to last night's dream. Down in the tracks, running from the trains, the dream relentless, never-ending. Maybe it's time you saw the doctor about all this. Take a morning off, a couple hours even. Maybe next week. But so little time. Fuck it anyway. You bring the cup to the bedroom, start to get dressed. Almost toppling as you pull on your trousers and cursing every cunt and bastard to hell. Jesus. Hands shaking as you fix your tie. Fuck this, you bring your coffee out to the cabinet and in goes a measure of vodka, a generous one, because God if you don't calm your nerves you're going to throw something against the wall. Fucking kill somebody. Seriously. You can see it. Donaldson at work, nothing ever good enough, jump over the desk, strangle the bastard to death on the floor.

But you've got to cool it. Get a move on. You down the coffee-vodka and collect up everything you need. Check yourself in the hallway mirror, make sure you've got everything, patting yourself down . . . phone, wallet, fags, keys, check your breath, your armpits, run back to the bathroom, more spray, back to the room, double check. Go on, fuck off, get to work.

You head for the door. And you can forget about drinks with McCluskey and Logan tonight as well – they're earning a lot more money than you, in a different league, stop embarrassing yourself. I mean, standing there with a pint in your hand laughing and joking, pretending everything's normal? That's you all over, isn't it. Just not getting it.

Go on, fuck off, get out of here. You move, heading out the door and down the path. And no pubs. I mean it, I want you straight home. Me and you, nice little chat. Are you listening to me? Fucking better be. We haven't even scratched the surface yet. Prick. Door slams and you shudder. Up your pace.

JIM, ONE OF A KIND?
Ian Bradley

Jim jumped out of bed just as his alarm went off. After a smooth, five-blade shave and a warm shower, he was fresh and ready for the day. He dressed himself in his neatly ironed clothes and scurried downstairs for breakfast.

The sun was beaming through the kitchen window and he couldn't contain his happiness. He munched on brown buttered toast washed down with a mug of black coffee. The last two days had been terrible. Every so often, he had to bear these two days, and they often made him quite ill.

After locking his house, he got into his car, started it up and sped along the roads, amber-gambling twice as he sang along to the joyful tunes on the radio.

Jim was ecstatic, brimming with confidence. He parked his car and hurriedly got out. Then, in a jog, he headed towards the door of the building, whistling. On opening the door, the machine made a tuneful ting and he smiled at the ticket like it was a six-number lottery winner: JIM MCGARRITY, MONDAY 14th MARCH, START TIME: 07:47.

HELLO
Kevin Tosca

'I'm not a lumberjack or fur trader and I don't live in an igloo or eat blubber or own a dogsled and I don't know Jimmy, Sally or Susie from Saskatchewan, although I'm sure they're really, really nice. I have a prime minister, not a president. I speak English and French, not American, and I pronounce it about, not aboot. I believe the beaver is a proud and noble animal. A toque is a hat. A Chesterfield is a couch. Canada is the second largest land mass, the first nation of hockey, and the best part of North America. My name is MARK and I am Canadian!'

Mark is 45 years old. He is a director. He has procreated. He makes roughly $150,000 a year.

Razur Cuts interviews
SLEAFORD MODS

Sleaford Mods first popped up on our radar in 2013 when we stumbled across 'Fizzy' on YouTube.

Jason Williamson (lyrics) and Andrew Fearn (music) are producing something truly original in an era where this is almost impossible. Finally, a band saying things we've been thinking for years, mixing politics with sharp, funny lyrics.

The band tours regularly and our beloved British public has finally caught on. We caught up with Jason (JW) in August 2016 for a chat.

RC: **Tell us how the band started, how you acquired your name and a bit about the early days?**

JW: I started it in 2006 I think, or 2005-ish. It was a studio project for a year and then I started gigging it. Took a while, cos I couldn't figure out if I was onto something or not. The name was a random idea in the pub relating to my childhood location(ish) and my liking for the mod thing. The early days were hard, fruitless and often utterly depressing, but that's how it goes.

RC: **What was the turning point when you became a two-piece and do you feel more pressure on stage due to there being no backing band?**

JW: The turning point was meeting Andrew and our boss Steve, and then releasing *Austerity Dogs*. No, I don't feel pressure at all with having no 'band'. The modern band today is mostly fucking useless. We're offering a different idea.

RC: **Your lyrics are hard hitting, meaningful and humorous. Which bands or lyrics influenced you?**

JW: Loads. Hip hop, punk, grime, too many to mention.

RC: **Do you see yourself as a writer or songwriter, and what inspires you to write?**

JW: Yea, course I do. It's music, isn't it? Life inspires me to write. The day-to-day. The dross. The humour.

RC: **Growing up, we had The Clash, The Jam and The Sex Pistols. Why do you think young bands don't have that fire, anger, angst and lyrical content of those aforementioned bands? Or is it just that we're not getting access to them?**

JW: There's some stuff that's trying to exist currently, but mainly it's wank money projects hiding behind reheated images.

RC: **We've heard from other artists that the music business is full of difficult people. Do you agree?**

JW: Yea, it can be, but there are some good people too. You choose to be a wanker, you aren't born one.

RC: **It must be so draining on stage for you, because you're so powerful and aggressive. Does it take its toll? Do you use a lubricant . . . for your throat?**

JW: No, I exercise every day. I don't booze anymore, no drugs either. Fuck all that, I did my time. I eat well too and that carries me. Also, voice exercises and a lot of thinking.

RC: ***Key Markets* is a stunning album. How did you feel when Iggy Pop voted it his album of 2015?**

JW: Fuckin great. He watched us in Helsinki at the side of the stage. Fuckin mad, innit? He's a saint. One of the last Titans.

RC: **Tell us about *Lost Dog*, the short film you star in. How did that come about?**

JW: *Lost Dog* was an idea born from the hateful policies of Tory rule relating to welfare and disability cuts, and it centres on one individual trying to survive as a result of those cuts being made. The idea was created by the actor/activist Andrew Tiernan. He came to a few gigs and we got talking. I've always been interested in acting as a creative thing, so it came from that really.

RC: **A prosthetic limb bounced onto the stage during a gig in Edinburgh in November 2015. It's the only time I've seen you lost for words. What was going through your mind at that point?**

JW: I was a bit stunned. Then worried it might get lost in the crowd as I assumed it belonged to a real limb!

LANE CLOSED
Jason Williamson

This country has the same kind of dour colour that Nigel Farage has. In his attire and hair, his tobacco-soaked skin. I know he's an easy target for those not consumed by this renascent bump in fascism, but touring the UK it occurred to me that it really is actually fucking shit beyond belief, isn't it? I don't think there is anything remotely attractive that I can store into my memory bank, perhaps the small wild forest sanctuaries that I glimpse through the windows of the tour bus stay with me and the gigs were wicked of course, but so fucking what. It occurred to me that like the referendum, the darkness lurks in the small cities, in their medieval monuments and slim streets. The never-ending screaming insecurities of eventless-ness. The potential for the old English demon will always be there too, the high street in almost every town is shut down apart from the eateries and coffee chains, which isn't exactly news, but even so, to see it over and over again from gig to gig makes it prick constantly in my thoughts. There is this dull silver sheen to everything, business suit grey. Farage trending on Twitter and for absolutely nothing. The Brexit Party? Fuck off, it's nothing. He is the Premier Inn of English politics, a miserable pool of lost minds and sausages. It's a shit hot dog, isn't it? A burger microwaved. Crap ¾ length cargo pants in tan. Every stranger looks terrible, people-watching is the mixing spoon to my mind's caldron of hate. Costa, JD Sports,

Wagamama, bubble buildings puking out gym bodies in Nike and Moncler and I'm no fucking exception either.

TATTOOED BRITS ON HOLIDAY
Peter MacDonald

With their lobster-like skin and protruding large guts,
Their loudmouthed girlfriends with their considerable butts,
Here they all are on their package holiday,
Reminding the world that Britain has had its day.

It's ink, ink, ink, both male and female,
Like a tattoo parlour fire sale,
You spend half the day aghast at what you see,
Secretly wondering *what the fuck is that meant to be?*

Football club badges and shit Chinese lettering, it's all on show,
Every square inch covered and every one a new low,
You start to feel out of place that you don't have one,
Then you remember to be different can be fun.

Masses upon masses of tattooed shit Brits,
Oversized women with crap ones on their tits,
Before, British nationality was a knotted hanky on your head,
Now you just wish the age of shit inking was dead.

THE DAILY MALE
J.A. Welsh

Here he comes in his fake Stone Island gear
Snide as fuck, spitting 'you shouldn't be here'
He's rampant, ridiculous, rarely on tact
A rank rotten racist, always on the attack

Brexit means Brexit, that was his vote
Close the borders, scuttle the boat
Subordinate, dominate, know your place
An apron, an empire, he wants one race

Fool Britannia, he's media-led
Fake news, what does it mean to be a red?
Suck it up, lap it up, it's beyond the pale
The Daily Mail, the daily male

His right wing rhetoric is dragging him down
His right wing rhetoric is dragging me down
His right wing rhetoric is dragging you down
His right wing rhetoric is dragging us down

NORMALLY
Ian Cusack

Good afternoon, guy! My name is Mrs. Bob Wood from the United Kingdom. My wife is called Kazakhstan & we live in the United Kingdom. My wife is a philanthropist, she encourages me to help poor people. I want you to know that I did not just wake up & decide to contact you.

Normally, it's pretty monotonous nearby me, but shortly ago I did have the occasion to participate in an interesting multiracial bed game, where double intrusion was really like baby performance against to what these people did to my forms! All happened 2 days ago. I certainly never had so fantastic & such unique life experience. All my very own lovable hollows were petted & outstretched. I were extremely worn-out after that. I realise that in fact, I definitely like night times & night exercises. Oh, those adult activities were undoubtedly spectacular! I've never felt so free & inspired, even made a private home video & a big amount of pix when I'm dressed just in very small bikini. I really want 2 show you a few photos in my little clothing, & possibly even devoid of any clothes & I do not know any reasons why a fine fellow must hide your big joystick from me.

My form is remarkable & eye-catching, I've an athletic slip-shape & great bum with tits. I definitely like it when my boobs are touched. I impatiently want u to pet my wet kitty, grab me on da desk. I expect you to take me in all positions, my precious, with no other responsibilities. I wish to have these games regularly & for a very long time! I will caress u with my strong fists & will love you pretty smoothly during all night.

Try to reply to me immediately for more information. May God bless you & your family. I would love to talk to you on the phone, but the problem is that I do not know your language & cannot speak well due to pains. Please keep this information very secret, for security reason.

Looking forward to hearing from you urgently. Mail me!

Razur Cuts interviews
JOHN ROBB

John Robb (JR) is a music journalist, musician and original member of punk band The Membranes. He is also the founder and boss of monthly music magazine *Louder Than War*. He gave up some of his precious time in the summer of 2018 to chat to us.

RC: **Tell us about your journey from the founding member of a punk band in 1977 to running a music magazine.**

JR: That's a very long journey! When we started, we were captivated by the energy and empowerment of punk rock and formed a band. We had no idea how to play and I made a bass guitar out of a piece of driftwood from the beach and the neck of a Woolworths bass guitar! When we went on stage we thought tuning up was putting all the machine heads in a row! We had never even played through amps before the first gig and made up chords and scales of our own because there was no way of learning. It was classic DIY.

In a weird way, this was always very much the spirit of the band . . . making music on our own terms. Making sense out of chaos. Even to this day, having learned exactly how to do what we do, we still operate beyond the bounds of convention, but somehow it works and pieces of music and songs make sense to us and the audience, which is very exciting! I think this kind of thinking was typical of that post-punk period . . . when I speak to Peter Hook he always tells me that he can't play covers and can only play his own bass lines – which he has honed to personal perfection – and this is something we do as well. It was the fascinating thing about that period . . . really unlikely people spurred on by the energy of punk to get up and play – and it defined post-punk. That was the period when teenage fans had a go with no prior musical knowledge – and out of their wonky musical backgrounds, they created something truly original, not trapped by the tried and tested ways of making music. They created something magical in far flung towns with no local music scene to tag onto.

These days I work with choirs and sometimes strings and the same rules apply. I have to sing the parts at them and wave my arms around until it makes sense. I trust my own instincts and make music that feels right. It can either be there to create a mood or a rush of adrenalised energy, as I like dark atmospheres, but also still love that rush of excitement of music born out of growing up in punk.

Back to the question, we also did a fanzine called *Rox* and were very much part of that bricolage cut and paste Xerox generation. From there I drifted into the music press care of *Zigzag* in 1983 and then *Sounds*. Meanwhile, the band became a big cult band with the support of John Peel and the music press and we went deep into a very noisy, discordant place which, oddly, seemed to have influenced a lot of American bands that we always get told we were influenced by! Very confusing. After that I did a stint as Goldblade and more and more writing with my own website *Louder Than War,* which is also a magazine . . . this potted history doesn't even scratch the surface really, but I rarely look back at the "good old days".

RC: **How important is it for a band to evolve? Many bands have gone through an evolution process and many haven't. Do you think some don't – or can't – because they love their original sound, or just feel comfortable playing the same style? Or do you think the creativity in an individual or group of musicians leads to an inevitable change, both lyrically and musically?**

Fans can be the same, like they're being disloyal to their favourites if they like different genres and bands. We feel that, as we get older, we're listening to a wider range of stuff – and really enjoying it!

JR: I think different bands operate in different ways. Bands like Swans, Einsturzende Neubauten and The Fall were built for change and part of the thrill of liking those bands was their constant evolution; that's a constant evolution we are part of. Our music changes a lot but is still built around fundamentals, like the bass guitar will play many of the lead lines whilst the guitars don't play solos but make great noises or textures, or play chopping rhythms whilst the drums play tight, repetitive, hypnotic patterns with me delivering surreal wordplay over the top. The upcoming album will also have choirs singing drones or melancholic parts over this. I played one of the new songs to Andy from Therapy? and he told me he thought it sounded like a Hieronymus Bosch painting! What a perfect description!

Meanwhile, the other bands that I love, like The Stranglers, are great when they play those magical hits with a dusting of new stuff. Those hits were signposts to our adolescence and important songs in our lives!

The changes in The Membranes' music are because of the sheer volume of possibilities hinted at by other music or just knowing how to make the sounds that are in your head and daring to do them. The last album was a double album about the universe and my father dying, and the new album is about the chaos and beauty of nature and the inevitability of life and death, and is threaded with Brexit and broken love and lust. The empowerment of punk meant that there was never any fear of tackling the big subjects!

Personally, my music taste is very wide these days, from drone rock to African music to dub to punk to, well, nearly everything. Punk is still very important to me – its attitude as how I perceived it all those years ago is very much the core of everything.

RC: **We saw you in our local town with The Membranes and the band blew us away. Unbelievable energy levels. You keep yourself extremely fit and healthy. Take us through a day in the life of John Robb from when you get up in the morning.**

JR: I think that when you make physical music, you have to present it in a very physical way. I keep myself fit so I can embrace the physicality of the music. It can't be played in a chair! My body is bent out of shape and buffeted by the music. The next day there are bruises but I don't feel it in the middle of the intensity of performance and that deep physical and mental entrancing is such a big attraction to performing!

Our music may not all be four-to-the-floor wham bam and we do have some quite psychedelic drone drop downs but when we mount the wild beast we really feel the lift-off! It's amazing how much of a lift music can give you. It's the ultimate art form. Watching a band is far more engaging than being slumped at home watching TV. That shuddering primal power and almost animal-like craziness on stage is the ultimate aim of the music for me. It's transcendental. Like a punk rock shaman!

I get up at about 8am and try and answer as many messages as I can, but there can be too many! If I'm in Manchester, I'll spend the morning writing or editing my book or website, the afternoon trying to organise stuff online because I'm the manager of the band, and then I go to the gym to try and clear my head. I train intensely and it feels great – a body is not built for an armchair, it's meant to be physical. We were built to push mammoths off cliffs – although as a vegan I've evolved beyond that bit, but my body still needs the physical kick! In the evening, I go and see bands play. Manchester is great for this. I live on the edge of the city centre and there are 40 venues within ten minutes' walk or cycle of my flat.

Many days I'm not in Manchester though – these days I'm fortunate enough to get flown into Europe to talk about music at lots of different events in places like Portugal, Poland, Slovenia, Russia, Germany and Holland. I'm in London a lot too, and also running my 'In Conversation' event *Louder Than Words* in Manchester every November . . . so a lot going on!

RC: **You're from Blackpool, a place many people visit as a holiday resort. What was it like seeing different faces every day on the street? Is there still a sense of community in the town? Like us, you fervently support your local football team. We were in Blackpool in 1981 on holiday. Spray painted on the wall outside Bloomfield Park was, "We'll support you ever more, even in division 4"! We've never forgotten this. Did you write it?**

JR: Ha ha, that slogan is somehow so British, so dogged and sad. Blackpool was a schizophrenic place to grow up – on one level it was this weird Day-Glo funland with millions of people going crazy with their "I shot JR" hats and fake dog leads and whatever bric-a-brac they had been flogged at the time. It could get pretty violent as some people seemed to think attacking the local punk rocker was part of the holiday fun. All the pubs were geared towards tourists, so we would be endlessly thrown out of pubs for not dressing correctly.

On the other hand, it was also a normal town . . . it's quite a big place – bigger than people think, so there was also a sense of normal town life. There was a good community on the local punk scene with many really good bands, like Section 25, whose debut album was released by Factory and as an album is as good to me as the Joy Division debut – please go and listen to it – both albums are produced by Martin Hannett. There were also quality punk bands like The Fits and One Way System and then there was The Membranes, who were the misfits as ever. But punk was a broad church so we were part of the scene and documented it with our fanzine, *Rox*.

Another factor was that the town could be very bleak in the winter – the wind howling across the town and the waves crashing onto the promenade, carrying piles of strange-looking seaweed and deep sea animals' corpses in its wake. But I totally loved that bleakness; the creaking and droning, and the screeching of seagulls. Much of that would make its way into our music, enhanced by the magic mushrooms we would take in the autumn. It's those sounds that reflect the fierceness of nature and the way that at the bottom of my road the man-made suburbia would suddenly end in the dark void of the crashing ocean. It made me feel invigorated on one level and small and frail and human on another. I could physically see the boundary between the thin veneer of civilisation and the eternal thundering ocean; the power of nature. That is part of the upcoming album as well.

RC: **What's the most rewarding thing that's happened to you since forming or reforming The Membranes and being boss of *Louder Than War?* All the magazines we grew up with are disappearing. What were your ideas and intentions at the beginning of your magazine?**

JR: The most rewarding thing for The Membranes was being able to come back and release the *Dark Matter/Dark Energy* album. This has been our best received and best selling, which is something that should never have happened. It has also been rewarding to be able to be so ambitious with the band and make our own music under our own rules, which is something we've always liked. The next album will continue in this vein with many tracks having a choir on them and being darker and even more epic than *Dark Matter/Dark Energy*, but with the best driving bass sound I've ever concocted.

I was surprised by the success of the magazine. Print can struggle, but somehow the magazine does better and better and has survived when many others have disappeared. I'm not saying it's easy though! I'm not against change and love many aspects of the internet; for a start, it's given underground bands a platform to get their music out and not to be so marginalised by the mainstream. It's great to see bands like Idles do so well – that could only have happened with the internet and an underground network spreading the word until the mainstream could no longer ignore them.

RC: **When you reformed The Membranes, was the intention just to play the All Tomorrow's Parties festival for Kevin Shields of My Bloody Valentine as a one-off, or did you feel quickly that you still had something to say and, more importantly, new music to make?**

JR: It was only for a one-off but it went well, so we did a couple more and then I decided The Membranes was never meant to be band looking back, so we recorded a double album of new stuff. The music is always pouring out and there are so many ideas to be tried and finished off. The next album is very diverse, from gnarly to epic, from beautiful drones to cranked post-punk.

RC: **Tony Wilson is a sadly missed Manchester enigma. Tell us a story about him we might not know. Also, why are loads of great bands from the Manchester area or Scotland?**

JR: Tony was a lot nicer than he would like you to think. Of course he was abrasive and loved debate, but he genuinely cared about people. I would bump into him nearly every day as he lived near me and his flat was on my route back from the gym, and we'd have some good debates about music. No matter how intense they got, he would never fall out with me and loved the verbal jousting. I never thought of myself as part of his inner circle though, so I was surprised when I was invited to his funeral and was told that I was one his favourite people in town. The funeral was the last Factory number in the catalogue and was a pop culture moment . . .

they played Joy Division's 'Atmosphere' at the funeral and it was very moving and gave the song a whole new meaning for me.

I think the big former industrial cities like Manchester and Glasgow were always harsh but melodic. That post-industrial space created a void of broken warehouses and cheap spaces where art and music could be made, and for many people it was a chance to create magic in the desolation. Of course, this has all changed now and these are cities that, on the surface, are booming with rebuilt centres, but music has become part of the identity of these places and it's one of the things that people do. It's also a chance to deal in art, poetry and emotion in places where sometimes these things had to be hidden behind a tough facade! Also, mad cities are full of wild-eyed genius!

RC: **After reading Razur Cuts, you've been extremely complimentary. What advice can you give us for the future of the magazine? Our ethos stands firm on not having the content of our editions online, as we want to be traditional, like punk fanzine *Sniffin Glue*. As the grandmaster, please give us your opinion on this.**

JR: I like online and don't believe there's a right or a wrong. What worked in 1977 might not work now. On the other hand, I am a big supporter of any alternative media. I don't want to get talked down to by a cosy media elite even if some of those people are brilliant at what they do. For me, the voice in Falkirk is as important as the voice in

London. I'm fascinated by people's lives and how music is ingrained in them. I love fanzines where I can hear that person's voice, a voice in the wilderness and how they react to the culture. I used to love stuff where it became almost like a diary – that romantic quest for art and culture in broken towns!

I like the way your fanzine looks good and has long-form articles in it. I love a good, solid, long read and in-depth interviews. Whether this is as print or online, I don't mind – it's the words that mean everything to me more than what they're presented on, but there is still something powerful about holding a magazine or a book. It's like a whole universe of words to get lost in in your hands.

Derek S

Gordon Whyte

PLANNING A COMEBACK
David F. Ross

He says sorry, before a warm hello.
A mellow sound in accelerating flow
phrasing from a smooth to staccato riff.
Worn leather, grey smoke and Brylcreemed quiff.

Addictive enthusiasm, sparkling eyes,
he speaks like Dylan; rhythm and surprise.
It soars, dips, calms and beguiles,
magnetic, entrancing, Lord of these aisles.

Out into stair rod rain, a saunter.
Victorian streets. Earthquake Weather.
We talk about going missing in '82 –
cryptic, jousting, he offers no clue.

On stage, the indignant fury returns.
Words hitting targets. Bullets from a gun.
A ballroom crescendo. A familiar scene.
Arms aloft. Leopard-skin Limousines.

Thirty years pass, I think of him still.
The mellifluous voice, the anger, the thrill.
Writing new songs, recording on 8-track,
out in the desert; planning a comeback.

ACTION MAN ISN'T COMING BACK
Stephen Watt

Candlesticks, headphones, bike reflectors, cell phones,
crack pipes, cotton balls, coloured pencils, Barbie dolls,
toy wands, scented soap, deodorant cap, dominoes,
coke bottles, dumbbells, prosthetic eyeballs.

Explain that one to the hospitals.

Frozen hot dogs, light bulbs, chess piece, a ripe banana,
a shot glass, nail files, a Wi-Fi router antenna,
toothbrush, drumsticks, cigarettes and lighter,
remote controls, dildos, a Donny Osmond poster.

Explain that one to the doctor.

Vibrator, turkey baster, perfume bottle, coat hanger,
screwdriver, rock salt, earbuds, condom wrapper,
fidget spinner, plastic spider, action figure, laser pointer,
tape dispenser, egg timer, plastic sword, thermometer.

Your reasons are you didn't want to disappoint her.

Microchip, bits of puzzle, half a buttered bagel,
juice box straw, water gun, plunger handle,
a drill bit, a stuffed bird, wood chip, a piece of bed,
detergent pod, hearing aid, folding knives and razur
blades.

Shall I play nursemaid?

Razur Cuts interviews
MARTIN GEISSLER

Martin Geissler (MG) is best known for his work as a TV reporter and Journalist for ITN News. He is now one of the presenters on the BBC Scotland's flagship news show *The Nine*. We caught up with Martin in August 2020 to discuss his TV career, Trump and his love for music.

RC: **Tell us a bit about how you got started in journalism.**

MG: When I was about 13, I was on the Janice Long radio show taking part in a quiz called *Select-a-Disc*. From memory, if you got a question right you got a single and you could gamble it for an album token. We had a little chat at the end and she said, "What do you want to do when you leave school?" I told her I wanted to be a journalist. I then lost that idea a bit because I didn't know how to become a journalist, and certainly not a TV reporter!

I left school and travelled for a while to try and get my head straight. I had done just enough to get into university but had missed the entrance dates and had time to kill, so enrolled with a couple of recruitment agencies. One of them called and said Edinburgh Zoo wanted an office junior in their press office. I got the job and did it for nine months. The job was primarily punting pictures of baby animals to newspaper picture editors on newspapers, defending the zoo to animal rights organisations and writing press releases. Because we did press calls there, I also got to meet a lot of journalists.

The time came to go to uni but someone from Sky News, which had just started, told me they needed an assistant in their bureau for a few months. I decided to see if I could hack it and loved it. I was there for two years. Nothing had really clicked in my life – I didn't know what I wanted to do, but suddenly this made sense. I lost my job there because Sky had to make cutbacks, so I wrote to every single TV newsroom in the country. I got a job covering maternity leave for Grampian TV and stayed there for nine months, then went to Tyne Tees in Newcastle for more maternity leave cover. While I was there, the boss at Scottish TV saw my tape and said there was a reporter's job going in Edinburgh with occasional reporting, so I took that and stayed for four years.

I then went to Sky Sports for 18 months because I thought it would be good fun, before returning to STV. Then ITN's Scotland correspondent left and I got the job of covering while they looked for a replacement. However, I got my foot in the door and four years later became their Africa correspondent, then Euro correspondent, and then came home. Scotland is like golden handcuffs; you can't ever properly leave it as it's too good. I was fortunate enough to then get a role covering special interest and international reports for *News at Ten* and was with ITN for 17 years.

RC: **You worked in the Sates in the build-up to Trump being voted in as the 45th president. Can you tell us a bit about your time there?**

MG: I spent weeks in the States in the run up to the election. I got it quite wrong. I stood up on *News at Ten* in front of millions of people and said "Be certain of this. Donald Trump will not win the Republican nomination, never mind be the president. He won't even be their candidate." But then as the election got closer, I realised he was going to win.

I was in Youngstown, Ohio – a proper steel town, which Springsteen wrote a song about. It's like ground zero for blue collar democrat supporting working class Americans, a real rust belt town. The thought was that if Trump can turn here, then all bets are off.

When we got there, a week away from the polls, we spoke to one guy and asked him what he was thinking. He said, "What am I thinking? I am thinking there are 350 million people in this country, and they are asking us to choose between these two". In one sentence, he nailed how the majority of the country was thinking.

There was no great love for Trump other than his own base, but a lot of people voted for him with no great joy. What we didn't get here in the UK was the true extent of the antipathy towards Hilary Clinton because she represented the entitled dynastic politics that the States has known for so long. Now, an entitled New York property billionaire is the least likely guy to fight for the working folk but it just shows you that if you've got the message, you can sell it.

RC: You've also worked as a foreign correspondent. What would you say have been the stick-out moments?

MG: I covered Hurricane Katrina, the Asian tsunami, the second Iraq War, Afghanistan, the Libyan revolution, the migrant crisis, all of that. There are two things that live with me. I was in Baghdad in 2003, staying in the Palestine Hotel and woke up as a massive bomb went off. The windows of the hotel shook as the Jordanian Embassy had been blown up. This was Al Qaeda's first incursion into Iraq. We went over to the embassy and it was a brutal scene. A suicide bomber was in pieces on the wasteland outside. I had never seen anything like that in my life.

About two weeks later, a cement mixer laden with explosives drove into the UN compound and blew the place to bits. Twenty-three people were killed. We drove in before the cordon went down and watched a guy being brought out on a stretcher by two American soldiers. He died just by us. The soldiers put the stretcher down, took their helmets off and then walked back to get the next guy. For some reason, that's the one I see in my dreams sometimes. It was brutal.

The other one that has stayed with me happened during the migrant crisis. People were coming across a small channel of water of only about four miles between Turkey and Lesbos on boats to put their feet on European soil before heading on to Munich.

I suggested to the editor that we should follow them and file a piece a night – so report the first night from the beach in Lesbos, the second night from the Macedonian border, then on to Serbia, then Austria and finish in Munich – weirdly enough, we reached Munich on the night the Bataclan was bombed. What sticks in my mind was standing on a beach in Lesbos. The cameraman felt he hadn't properly captured the gut-wrenching scene of these people crawling out of the boats. He had photographed it from a distance but didn't feel he was doing it justice.

We drove up to a clifftop from where we could see a lot of boats landing. It got dark and he said he could see a light in the distance like a pin prick. "I think that's a raft," he said, so we drove off the clifftop and down to the beach. As we ran along the pebble beach, we could hear screaming and suddenly we saw the raft with 80-year-old people, women with tiny babies . . . these people were waist deep in water, sobbing and gagging and it was a while before I realised I was standing on the beach powerless, crying my eyes out.

It was the emotional intensity of that moment and realising what they had been through. Of all the stuff I've seen and experienced, that's the only time I really lost it, and it was a moment where I wouldn't have thought I would have, but it was incredibly profound.

We spoke to a woman on that raft who was with her husband and her five-year-old kid and I said to her, "How can you put your kid through that?" She gave me both barrels and it was amazing. I had asked the question so I could help people understand the situation, and she responded, "Do you think I would put my child at risk because I wanted to? We have no choice. We are running from Assad, we are running from IS, who are brutalising people, we are running from a war that is reducing our city to rubble and we have absolutely nowhere to go. It's this or die. Imagine that for a second and ask me what you would do?"

RC: **Tell us how you came to work on the BBC Scotland show, *The Nine*?**

MG: The BBC were starting a project which was to be an hour of Scottish news from an international base, going out at nine o'clock. The opportunity came up to present it and I was keen to take up a new challenge because you can be a half-decent reporter, but that doesn't mean to say you'll be any good as a presenter. It's a completely different thing.

    The programme has an identity now and we're developing it. I love presenting on it because at the start I could be interrogating the First Minister – and there has never been a more important time to be questioning the people who run Scotland – and at the end, I could be talking to the entertainment correspondent about Coronation Street! It's my dream job.

RC: **What kind of music are you into, both currently and from the past?**

MG: Music has always been a passion of mine. I still go back to The Clash, The Damned and The Sex Pistols – they grabbed me when I was about 13. I felt intoxicated by *Never Mind the Bollocks* because it had bad language. It was fast and loud and amazing, and every song on that album still stands up. When I was ten, it was all about Adam and The Ants. The first record I remember actually buying was *Parallel Lines* by Blondie. I saw The Damned at The Playhouse when I was 14 and then I got into psychobilly. I saw The Meteors at The Music Box in Edinburgh, that was quite a night. I loved all the Psychobilly stuff – Guana Batz, The Polecats, The Milkshakes and The Coffin Nails.

Music came up in conversation in a strange way for me a few years ago. I was in Afghanistan, camped out with some US marines and we were sitting around a fire. I had my phone lying next to me but with no data or Wi-Fi and these guys were talking about bands. They were all into hard rock and said, "Aw, you had some great British bands," and I said, "Yeah, you are going to tell me you like Iron Maiden in a minute." So we were laughing about it and I must have said Iron Maiden about half a dozen times, as when I was about 13, everyone was into Iron Maiden but I hated them.

The next day, I got onto Wi-Fi. Now, I've never bought an Iron Maiden record, I've never spoken about them from the age of 13 until that night, but the first thing that happened when I got onto Facebook the next day was an offer for an Iron Maiden sweatshirt! Don't tell me Facebook isn't listening to you . . .

Nowadays, I like Sleaford Mods. Jason is really inspirational – that anger and that total disrespect for what's gone before in the industry. I had heard some of their stuff, then I saw them on Jools Holland and they just blew me away. Fontaines D.C. I enjoy. Cait O'Riordan of The Pogues mentioned them on Twitter, so I clicked the link and they blew me away too. Their second album is reassuringly good. It's a departure and it's more mature.

For my 40th birthday, I had tickets for Primal Scream at Brixton Academy for my wife and me, but I ended up in Benghazi on the frontline of the Libyan revolution being shot at! That's how this line of work can screw things over!

WHEN IT ALL KICKS OFF IN FOREDYKE
Jim Higo

We don't give a toss about your revolution.
We lurch from shit jobs to futile fucks
Dragging our heels down deserted streets,
Bumming weed and weak lager outside abandoned shops.
We're doing time, slopping out the crap that laps up at our cell doors,
Staring at the same walls as our parents and their parents and their parents.
Today has ceased trading, it's been shut down and boarded up.
Tomorrow is derelict and waiting to be demolished.
We're looking for meaning in frightened faces.
What you say mate? What you say?
It's why Owen Jones will never understand why it all kicks off in Foredyke.

He's the hardest lad on the estate.
Ripped muscles bulging with steroids and stress.
He's looking for a place to unleash his paranoia
His head is a melting candle burning itself out with confusion.
His veins bulge and twitch from shared needles stuffed with shit gear and doomed ambitions.
Praying he'll be the one to learn his way out, or talk his way out, or fight his way out.

He wants to die in battle,
He wants to feel the thrill of staring down the barrel of a gun
He wants to make someone afraid.
You looking at our lass mate, you looking at our lass?
It's why it only takes a careless glance and it all kicks off in Foredyke.

We've forgotten how to dream,
We give our faith to gods who have stopped pretending they care.
We swing aimless punches at defenceless targets,
Passing our anger between us like an unpinned grenade,
Dumping our flea-bitten plans in someone else's dustbin.
We look for blame in different voices, different skins and different bodies
Until the only feeling left is hate.
And destroyed, we turn our hatred on each other,
And nobody notices and nobody cares.
You're not from round here are you mate, you not from round here?
And the riot van drives the other way when it all kicks off in Foredyke
It's 50 years of being ignored when it all kicks off in Foredyke
And they clean the mess and carry on when it all kicks off in Foredyke.

BLACK FLAG KINDA DAY
Bradford Middleton

Another shit day draws to a close at the hellhole known as work and again I'm grateful to just get out, out of there as soon after four as I can possibly move, as today has been a hard one, another day in a lifetime of misery spent being told off by customers and chastised by shoplifters.

One customer today shouted 'I am not your mate, I am a customer,' and after that torrent I thought of another few words I'd like to use to describe him. Then there were our usually prolific shoplifters, giro money fresh in their pockets, queuing up to actually buy their booze after being shouted at. 'Get to the back of the queue,' one of our braver, more vocal customers instructed as they swarmed around the checkout eyeing up a bottle to destroy their day.

When home came into view, I knew what I needed: some good old fashioned cathartic Black Flag, Henry Rollins screaming in my ear telling me exactly what I need to hear as the weed blazed away, making me calm and able to sit and write this rather than go to the pub to forget it all that way.

SEARCHING FOR ANSWERS
Martin Geraghty

Posing questions, like an inquisitive child,
searching for answers,
Dread and fear that we're fixed,
no scope for change,
A habitual sense of unease
orbits the solar plexus,
Demonic conspiracies arm in arm
with this elaborate nexus,

Shining a torchlight on the mechanics of mind,
searching for answers,
The fragility of optimism,
exposed, lay bare,
Kleshas force entry,
a demand for squatter's rights,
Nausea and agitation,
qualified providers, of sleep deprived nights

Blindfold in a labyrinth of esoteric conundrums,
searching for answers
Energy depleted,
diminished returns, hopes spurned,
'There's no such thing as depression!'
the keyboard warrior rants,
A modern fable, ladies and gentlemen,
welcome to 'bants'

The cessation of analysis,
no more searching for answers,
Uncomfortable friends, relationship dead-ends,
a brain that won't mend,
Letters of rejection,
feelings of neglect oozing from every pore,
Knife meets skin,
the endgame? blood and gore.

Razur Cuts interviews
RICHARD JOBSON

Richard Jobson (RJ) is a musician, writer and film director. He rose to prominence with punk band Skids in the 70s and new wave four-piece The Armoury Show in the 80s. These bands have now been resurrected and are still hammering home their panache 40+ years after their inception. His passion for the arts has taken him all over the world since his humble beginnings. He kindly gave us an interview in June 2019.

RC: **You wrote 'Into the Valley' at 15 years old. Can you remember the day you wrote it and everything that inspired the song? Did the music and lyrics fit immediately, or did the process take longer than anticipated?**

RJ: The lyrics were originally titled 'Depersonalised', which is not the catchiest, and evolved into 'Into the Valley'. I wrote the tune on the piano, which Stuart turned into a song. It came together really quickly after I showed him the words and played him the theme. The words have been criticised as being too abstract and a bit pretentious; I obviously don't agree. I remain very proud of the words and feel they remain relevant, especially with what is going on in the world.

RC: **Can you remember the first Skids get-together and practice? Were there line-up changes along the way, and could you feel chemistry developing before eventually being signed?**

RJ: The original line up never altered until the drummer left after the first album. I never understood why he left because the chemistry was good and the band were improving all the time, especially live. Our early practices were in an old garage and we used to get electric shocks all the time but it was an amazing experience being in a band and having a platform to air our views.

RC: **Songs like 'Working for the Yankee Dollar', The The's 'Heartland' and The Psychedelic Furs' 'President Gas' seem more relevant than ever. Thirty-five to 40 years later, we now find ourselves in a worse place. Will we ever learn?**

RJ: The song came back to me during the Iraq war. It made perfect sense and it was around that time that I started to think about Skids for the first time since we split and remember what we had achieved through our songs.

RC: **Your most enjoyable Skids album and why?**

RJ: I love *Days in Europa* because of its bravery and how we challenged ourselves to evolve as a band and as people. 'Animation' is a wonderful song. I also love the sleeve!

RC: You mentioned at your book launch that you were still a virgin when you appeared on *Top of the Pops*. One of Pan's People or Legs and Co took you home that night – is this true?

RJ: People tell me it's true, but I can't recall!

RC: **Please tell us how the brilliant Armoury Show came to fruition?**

RJ: It came about through Russell Webb and my friendship with John McGeoch. He was an amazing guitar player but had issues. The band was doomed. The album we made is great though. My favourite track is 'A Feeling'.

RC: **How did you find out about the sad passing of Stuart Adamson? It must have come as a great shock.**

RJ: It was and still is a shock. He was a great songwriter. We never fell out, remained in contact and shared some kind of friendship. He's missed by many, including me.

RC: **What were the major changes you noticed in the music industry after being away for so long? Did you need a period of adjustment to returning and playing live?**

RJ: Playing live is what I love most and Skids shows are very demanding and physical. But we deliver every time we play. The industry is unrecognisable and to be in a band these days you need wealthy parents.

This is not good news for young working class musicians, who are being frozen out.

RC: **You are cast as Alan McGhee's father in the biopic of McGhee's life, *Creation Stories*. Once you've directed, can you just act, or do you find yourself taking direction whilst biting your lip?**

RJ: It was great fun acting and I would like to do more. It was the route I chose at the end of Skids, but it was hard being a working class actor then – and still is now. The acting world is full of posh folk and most of the parts are designed for them. I have tried to change that in my movies. It was easy to take direction from a good director and that was definitely the case on *Creation Stories*.

RC: **Following a hearty meal, if you could sit down at a roaring fire, sipping a glass of expensive port, to talk music, who would you choose to be there and why? The artist can be dead or alive.**

RJ: Joe Strummer, Leonard Cohen, Lou Reed, David Bowie: they are parts of my life every day. And my life would be emptier without them and their music. They are icons in a shitty world and make my small world a bit better every time I listen to their music.

FINISHING OFF
Dickson Telfer

My mouth was shaped for a pint, so I was disappointed when Jerry returned from the bar with bottles of Beck's. They were ice cold though, just the ticket for such a scorching hot day. The back of my neck burned as Jerry squinted, occasionally using his hand as a visor. He's the only person I've ever known to never wear sunglasses; says he doesn't want panda eyes.

The taste reminded me of my first time drinking. Two Beck's and two Diamond White I had. Fourteen and buckled. I don't know if it was that, the novelty of drinking outside in nice weather, or the excitement of seeing Jerry for the first time in years, but even after a few sips I felt tipsy.

'Is it just me, or was that a bit weird back at the house?' I asked.

'Don't worry about it, mate,' said Jerry, squinting so hard it looked like he had no eyes at all, only black holes. 'She's had a few family issues recently, so she's a bit on edge.'

'Nothing too serious I hope?' I said, realising I sounded nosey rather than considerate.

Jerry clawed at the label on the back of his bottle. It came off easily, the condensation having loosened the gum. 'No, just a blip,' he said.

It had been difficult getting out of Jerry's house earlier. I had driven past the pub on the way there and had clocked the beer garden. I'd hoped it would be a quick turnaround, but his fiancé was reluctant to let him go. At one point I thought she was going to come with us, but Jerry must've sorted things out when they were whispering in the other room.

Back in the day, Jerry could make me piss myself laughing with just an expression, sometimes a single word, or even a well-timed pause. I'd never met anyone who could do comedy so subtly. Years ago I'd encouraged him to do stand-up, but he said there was a big difference between playing off me in familiar company and standing in front of an audience of strangers. I took it as a compliment: he was only funny because of me; without me feeding him, he was nothing.

'So how's the job going?' I asked.

'Yeah, alright,' he replied. 'Some of the guys I work with are tools, but the money's good, which is handy since I've got a wedding to pay for.'

I smiled. 'When's the big day again?'

'A year in July.'

I was waiting for something funny to follow, but nothing did. 'Cool,' I said. 'Looking forward to it?'

'Yeah, it'll be a good day,' he replied, running the nail of his thumb along the gummy residue where the label had been. The sun was so strong I couldn't tell if he was looking at me or not.

I'd met Jerry's wife-to-be for the first time about an hour before we'd left for the pub. "I've heard a lot about you," she'd said, shaking my hand limply, her palm creamy.

I wanted to ask if he had a best man in mind, but thought it wasn't the right time. I'd bring it up later after a few more beers.

'It's great to see you, mate,' Jerry said. 'Thanks for making the trip down.'

'Not at all, man,' I replied. 'It's been way too long.'

I was expecting a crap joke but with perfect delivery, something to do with cock length maybe.

'It sure has,' he nodded.

'So,' I said, taking a big gulp of Beck's, which was warming too quickly for my liking. 'What we doing tonight? Hitting the town, I take it?'

'Maybe,' Jerry muttered. 'Carla's preparing dinner, so we'll need to go back for that, then afterwards we can see how we feel.'

'See how we feel?' I blurted, jovially. 'Aw, come on, man, I'm only here for a couple of nights. You've got to show me the hot spots in your new home town. I've never been in this neck of the woods before. Let's get pissed and laugh all fucking night like we used to.'

'Yeah, it's not that I'm not up for that, mate, I am, it's just . . .'

His phone rang.

'Hi, honey,' he said, turning side on. I put a hand on the back of my neck and pictured it being pink, like a rare steak. Jerry was making regular nasally sounds, his lips closed and tense, like he was a bad actor being asked to pout. He began peeling the front label on his bottle, nail tearing through the word Beck's. 'Well, we're just finishing off our beers and then we'll come back.'

Finishing off? I was finishing off the first one for sure, but I wanted at least a couple more before dinner. And pints this time, none of this 275ml nonsense.

'Okay, bye honey,' said Jerry.

'Right, it's my round,' I said, standing up. 'What you having?'

'Look mate, I'm sorry, but we're going to have to go up the road.'

'What? We've only been here five minutes and I haven't seen you for years. I want to have a laugh.'

'Carla doesn't like being on her own,' he said. 'I don't really go out without her. In fact, this is the first time I've been out without her since I moved here.'

I was waiting for him revealing this was a prank, that the whole thing was staged – the lack of carry on; the creamy handshake; the phone call. I was ready to laugh; laugh so hard my belly would hurt.

But instead he finished his Beck's and placed the bottle on the table, among the shredded labels. 'We'll sort something out for later on,' he said, standing up. 'Are you coming?'

'No,' I said, looking up at him. He still had no eyes. 'No, I'm staying here.'

Then he was gone.

THE APPRENTICE
Will B

Iain Bradbury marched the young James Preston down to the shop floor to meet his new workmates and journeymen.

James had spent two years in basic training and was a tad nervous as he was now going to be working with men his dad's age to finalise his four-year apprenticeship.

The formalities of his national insurance number and tax code had been sorted with office manager Mr Bradbury, and it was now time to get down to the nitty gritty.

'The men will be at their tea break, son, so I'll take you down to the howf to meet them.'

'Okay, thanks,' said young James, whose overall zip was down, revealing his last gig t-shirt – The Cure: *Pornography*.

On opening the howf door, Bradbury was met with scowling eyes but James got a few smiles and approving nods as the men recognised that this young man in the pristine overalls was to become one of them.

A grey-headed, bespectacled man looked over the top of *The Racing Post* and said to James:

'You'll never cure pornography in here son, thurz aroond 40 buff books chynge hands daily in this fuckin place.'

'Eh, lads,' Bradbury began, 'this is young James Preston, he's just completed his first two years at training school and he's now here to do the final two years of his apprenticeship, before hopefully being kept on permanently.'

A few tradesmen nodded but most kept on munching sandwiches and slurping tea from mugs the size of small buckets – they'd seen many an apprentice come through the door.

An old man by the name of Billy Shaw ushered James to a seat next to the old electric oven and handed him a piping hot mug of tea from a battered copper urn.

James accepted the tea and looked into the cup – it was like tar and loaded with sugar – it looked awful.

Ah better fuckin drink this, he said to himself.

As Bradbury made his way to the door, young James stood up and announced he'd like to say something.

Bradbury was taken aback at this and quickly remarked, 'James son, just have your tea and relax.'

His words were met immediately with a retort from a man called Jock Paterson.

'Fuck up Bradbury, the laddie wants tae speak, an e's goni, so you're listening tae um tae,' Jock's voice thundered.

Bradbury was in no mood to disagree with this man.

Jock Paterson stood six feet, five inches tall with shoulders like a tight end from the New York Jets, a full head of black hair with beard to match, and massive black-as-coal eyes with a menacing stare.

Written on the back of his overalls in graffiti was the word YETI.

'On ye go son, whit wis yer name again?'

'James.'

'Aye, oan ye go, James.'

'Firstly, nice tae meet yeez aw, an whit Ah'd like tae say is this . . . Ah dinnae want tae hear ony ae ye askin if a've goat ony photies ae ma maw, or whit size ma sistur's tits ur. Or be sent tae the stores fur a long stand. Also,

Ah dinnae want ony ae yeez pishin oan ma leg in the showers afore Ah go hame at night.'

'James, James,' Bradbury interrupted, only to be cut down by The Yeti.

'Ah thocht Ah telt ye tae fuck up? Wur ye no listenin?'

'We aw ken aboot you, ye ken.'

Iain Bradbury had been reported for sexual harassment four months earlier.

He'd been seen dropping his pen under wee 19-year-old Mary McGarrity's desk and looking up her skirt, but only Mary herself knew exactly how many times this had happened. It was by pure chance that one day when Bradbury was in full bend to pick up his pen that he broke wind, thus alerting the office staff to exactly what he was up to.

The whole scenario was quickly quashed when Bradbury announced a few days later that there would be no Christmas bonus and told Mary on the quiet that he'd make her and her "prick of a brother" Jim's life hell. The office staff agreed that the whole thing was just some massive misunderstanding, and Bradbury got off scot free. Funnily enough, he managed to have full control of his pen after that.

What Bradbury didn't know was that The Yeti was going to make him pay for his actions. "All in good time" as he put it to the howf boys.

Bradbury was silenced as young James went on, nervously –

'Ma dad said Ah should jine the union tae, so can onybody help?'

'Ah'll sort ye oot there, James,' piped up Rab Munroe. 'Jist gie's yer address an that, son.'

'Thanks,' James smiled.

The Yeti moved towards the door as Bradbury again

tried to escape this cauldron of hate he was captive in. A size 12 steel toe capped boot now kept the door shut.

'Very good young man, but there's one last thing Ah need ye tae dae,' said The Yeti.

James swallowed hard in anticipation.

'Tell this fuckin beast tae fuck off back up tae his oaffice.'

'Eh, Ah cannae dae that.'

'Aye, yer daein it,' said The Yeti in a threatening tone.

James was now physically shaking, but composed himself to blurt out . . . 'Get yersel tae fuck up they stairs Bradbury, ya fuckin toad-faced little cock rocket.'

Just as the last word left James's mouth, the steel toe capped boot arrived back beside its partner and Iain Bradbury became a free man.

The howf was now filled with crazed laughter as The Yeti approached young James with an outstretched arm and shook his hand vigorously.

'Welcome tae oor world, son. You'll be working with me this week. By the way, how's yer sistur's tits these days?'

Debs Mullen

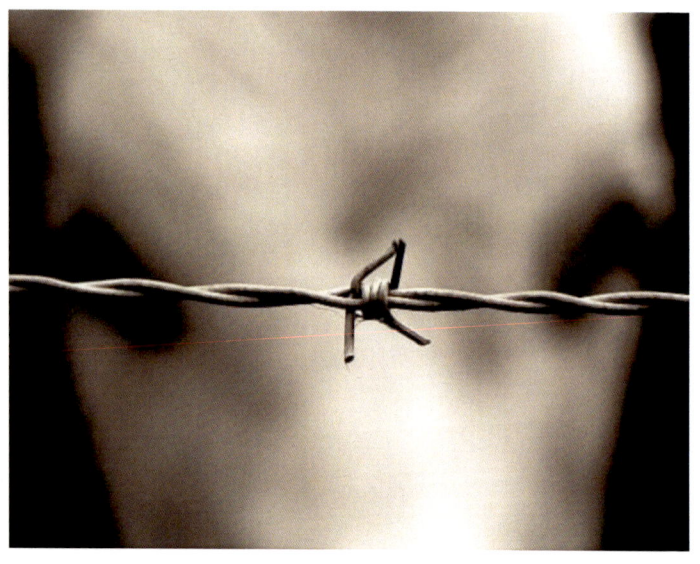

Gordon Whyte

Marcel Herms

Heather Scott

THE DREAM IS OVER
Mark English

January 1st, 1972

Paul: Hi John, it's Paul. Happy New Year. Do you fancy getting the band back together again?

John: Fuck off.

****

Sundays were always boring. None of the shops were open and there was nothing on TV worth watching. Sundays were when the schedules decided we should watch either religious programmes or ones about farming. As I'd never been to church and lived in the middle of a big city, neither held any appeal.

This Sunday though, in January, was even worse. It had rained since Christmas and I had no money to go for a drink even if the pubs were open. I flicked between the three channels and settled on *The Big Heat* – a black and white film on a bleak afternoon suited my black and white mood. The film was followed by the news. At least it'd soon be teatime and I knew we'd be having egg and chips. We always had that on Sundays for tea. Mam once presented us with PEK* and chips as a treat, but following universal dissent the chopped pork delicacy hasn't been seen since.

---

* a can of chunky pieces of cured chopped pork

I usually paid little attention to the news but tonight's lead story was different. I looked up to see an elderly man waving a white handkerchief whilst crouching over a body drenched in blood. Bricks were strewn across the road and others were being thrown as the sound of automatic rifle gunfire filled the living room. British soldiers were shown crouching behind cars, armoured vehicles trundling down the street, women crying, snotty-nosed kids with streaky faces and angry men. Lots of angry men. On both sides.

This is the UK. This is 1972.

WASTED VISTA, PART 0
Saira Viola

Blushing pink rushes the morning stars and silver-tipped whispers frown
on the drunken hiccup of pop dolls on heat
Thigh meets sigh for instant rub-a-dub-dub
Half-smoked cigarettes in-between lazy thighs
And fried grease promises say adios, farewell and goodbye

London plague isn't boiled red pestilence
It's a tea-coloured wheeze
from a choking weed
And a four-foot rat sucking on human meat

She managed on flat Coca-Cola
and sugar trails of larded MSG
Hers was the faded carpet misery
of dried out, shrivel-fucked austerity

Razur Cuts interviews
PAUL RESEARCH & SUKY GOODFELLOW

Paul Research (PR) was the guitarist in highly acclaimed Edinburgh post-punk band, Scars. They released one album, *Author! Author!*, as well as some much-loved singles. Since then, Paul has had many ventures – including the wonderful Voicex with Suky Goodfellow (SG) on lead vocals. Suky is also a member of the tremendous all-girl band, Fistimuffs. We met up with them in Leith Depot in the summer of 2018 for a wee blether and some real ale.

RC: **Scars played Grangemouth Town Hall in August 1978, supporting The Rezillos. That was our first proper gig, so this interview, 40 years later, is very special to us! What are your memories of that night?**

PR: It was a brilliant gig, but we received plenty hostility as we were playing outside Edinburgh. We had a good following in the city after gigging regularly, but when people don't know your stuff, they become frustrated and don't give you the chance. This tended to happen back then; they were behind the times. Sadly, there were anti-gay chants too, which was an indictment of life back in the 70s. However, it certainly wasn't the worst reaction we had. On a more positive note, two weeks later I received a letter from a pre-Cocteau Twins Liz Fraser saying how much she loved us. I still have the letter to this day. Great memories.

RC: **What was the approach when Scars signed to Fast Product Records?**

PR: It was an easy approach to be honest. Cockburn Street in Edinburgh had a record shop called Hot Licks. They had a bulletin board to advertise your band on. Many used it and it led to us asking for band members. Scars set up their own gigs back then. A kind of 'build it and they will come' approach. We had a gig in Balerno that Hilary Morrison organised for us. After coming to one of our rehearsals, she tried to raise a crowd by simply phoned people to tell them about the gig. It worked!

    Bob Last, owner of Fast Product Records, who managed The Rezillos, paid for our demos, which were recorded in Cargo Studios. We recorded our first single there too. Bob then had us supporting The Rezillos, which was a natural process as things progressed. We also supported The Human League and The Mekons, who are still friends. In the end, it was an easy signing. We concentrated on doing our own material and making it as good as we could.

RC: **The John Peel session – how were you contacted?**

PR: Once you have a record out on a label, you get opportunities to filter out. Same applies if you have a manager, booking agent etc. They contact others and have an interest in you getting work. Things tend to ramp up a good bit – record deals mean opportunities. Bob Last signed us to Fast Product and those opportunities arose regularly.

RC: **Was there a wilderness period when post-punk faded away and you stopped playing and rehearsing?**

PR: Yes, there was, but I never lost interest in music. I bought and learned the synthesiser and rehearsed at home. I also did the poetry circuit in London. Having done classical music on violin, grades six, seven and eight, I played with the Scottish Sinfonia in my early 40s, but electric guitar was really always my thing.

RC: **You joined Heavy Drapes. Tell us how this came about.**

PR: I was friendly with Richie, with whom I'd started Voicex, and he was already in Heavy Drapes. The band asked me to play one gig with them to help out on bass. I was totally into it, extremely enthusiastic. I thought they were a great band. Richie and I already had Voicex in the making, but there was no reason we couldn't do both.

RC: **What is the dynamic of Voicex and how did the band begin?**

PR: It started with Richie and I practising in the afternoons, then adding Coco as bass player. We thought we sounded good and aimed to do a gig with the intent on reaching out to different people, especially a young audience. It was then imperative to have a young singer who could engage with the audience. We had ideas of a girl rock gig. I asked Suky out of the blue if she'd join us and she immediately said yes. Suky and I share the lyrical content of our songs and she had such a backlog of material to use, so it all fitted easily into place.

SG: I do performance poetry too, so being the front person in the band was comfortable for me.

RC: **Suky, your voice is incredibly distinctive. Do you have a design or an approach to the way you want to sound?**

SG: No, not really, just to have passion and emotion in my performance as lead singer.

RC: **Have any of you thought of writing a book? Poetry perhaps?**

PR: I write daily. I give myself a task of 1500 words per day and I'm working on a book at the moment. It's hard work but challenging and enjoyable.

SG: I've written a book but it's unpublished as yet. Since I moved to Edinburgh five years ago my writing has elevated to another level.

RC: **The most important question of the interview now . . . is it roasted cheese, cheesy toast, cheese on toast or toasted cheese?**

PR: Roasted cheese.

SG: Cheese on toast.

RC: **What music are you listening to right now?**

PR: My playlist at the moment has Bowie, Ferry, Iggy and the classics. My live acts are Peter Cat from Glasgow, Fistimuffs and The Honey Farm.

SG: I love Dream Wife; they are very inspiring. I listen to The Pheromones and Tegan & Sara a lot too.

RC: **Suky, tell us about Fistimuffs?**

SG: We're an all-girl three piece based in Edinburgh and the name was taken from the word fisticuffs. I play guitar with co-vocals and we perform all our own material.

THANKS, DRIVER
Sophie McNaughton

As a taxi driver, Michael had seen it all. He took drunken teenagers home from house parties, asking if they were alright as they poured out of the backseat when he dropped them off. He took people to job interviews, weddings, funerals, christenings, court appearances and doctor's appointments. He helped people load their suitcases into his boot and took them to the airport in the wee hours for their holidays, enjoying the empty motorway and the summer night air flowing into the cab. He sat silently as couples had screaming, mascara-streaming breakups in the back seat and then a few days later new romances would start in the same place.

He was never short of stories.

'Did I tell ye about last weekend, Mick?' Craigy asked.

They were at the taxi rank underneath the bridge at Buckland Street. Michael always went back there between jobs on a Saturday night shift.

Michael cracked open a can of Coke. 'Ye did not.'

'Total nightmare, mate,' Craigy said. He produced a garage-bought pork pie from his jacket pocket, tore off the plastic and took a bite. 'It's about midnight, right? I gets a last-minute job for a pick up at The Crown, drop off up Hunterson Avenue.' Another bite. Crumbs fall down his front. 'Easy enough, right? Only a five-minute jaunt.'

Michael nodded and found himself brushing the front of his freshly-ironed shirt with his hand as if the crumbs were on him. He took another sip of his Coke.

'I wish I'd never taken it. It was a guy that phoned,' Craigy said, finishing his pie and chucking the wrapper back into his taxi. '"Just wanting a lift home, pal," he says. When I get there, he's standing ootside the pub. It's a nice wee boozer, The Crown, and he's finishing a fag and chatting away tae three other guys when I draw up. I sparked up myself and gave the guy a minute tae say cheerio.'

Michael's days were spent observing people, from the pedestrians he passed and occasionally beeped his horn at when they stepped out onto the road without looking, to the people who hailed him down in the rain and clambered into the warmth of his cab.

When he wasn't driving the taxi, Michael was at home, reading and listening to records with the occasional glass of wine. He'd never admit that to Craigy. Anything other than sinking pints and going to the bookies was alien to him.

'The guy's happy as Larry, ken?' Craigy said. 'Laughing away, pint in one haun, fag in the other. He's no even noticed I've drawn up. So, I just sit for a minute, listening tae the radio, thinking tae myself *I'll gie him a minute and then I'll wave tae get his attention.*'

Over the years, Michael felt he'd become somewhat of an expert on people, gauging within seconds if they would welcome his chat or his silence; he adjusted the service to each customer. He was endlessly fascinated at catching a glimpse of these strangers' lives, hearing their stories and wishing them well as he waved them off.

He found it to be a unique stranger-to-stranger encounter between punter and driver. Through the glass screen, people would willingly divulge little pieces of themselves, ending the exchange with a few extra coins in the tray over his shoulder and the sing-song of "Thanks, Driver".

'Well,' Craigy said, pausing for dramatic effect. 'The fella's face changes, right? He goes fae aw smiles and laughs tae this steely face, like lights oan but naebody's hame. But somebody's hame awrite. He drops the fag, right, and he lifts the pint glass, right up high, and smashes it doon on this other guy's heid a belter! Total carnage. The noise it made anaw. I was near boakin.'

Michael often found himself wondering about his customers. Did that woman in the blue suit get her big promotion? How did that old boy with the rosacea nose and walking stick get on visiting his wife up at the infirmary? He made peace with never finding out the answers but sometimes it still niggled at him.

'Ye wantae ah seen this, Mick,' Craigy said. Now that he'd finished his pie, it was time for dessert. A Mayfair. He pulled one from his packet and lit the end, taking a deep inhale that hollowed his cheeks and highlighted the shape of his skull.

'I mean, the gless smashes everywhere, right? Blood spewin fae the poor guy's heid, shoutin n bawlin. The guy hits the deck, clutching his heid, gaun, "Whit did ye dae that fur? Whit did ye dae that fur?" But the guy that's done it, the guy I'm meant tae be taking hame, is gaun aff his nut. The rest ae the guys back away. "We're no wantin any trouble, big man," and aw this.'

Michael nodded, urging Craigy to carry on. He stole a glance at the glove box in his taxi.

Craigy blew out a spiral of smoke. 'At this point, he clocks me,' he said. 'He geez me a wave. "I'll no be two seconds, pal," he says.'

Then he kicks the guy in the stomach, I mean he boots him right in the gut. I can practically hear the guy's insides crunching. It was awfy. Then he saunters over like nothing's happened and gets in the back seat. "How's yer night gaun, pal?" he says.'

Feeling that he should contribute to the conversation, Michael asked, 'What did you say to that?'

'Whit could I say? I wis in shock so I just started driving. I had tae ask the guy twice for the address, it kept gaun oot ma heid.'

Craigy took another deep draw from his cigarette and Michael watched the paper burn into a dangly tube of ash, itching to fall.

'I finally get tae ootside his hoose, longest five-minute journey of ma life. Then he tells me he's no got any cash oan him. By this point, I'm no even caring. I'm just wanting him oot, right?'

Michael nodded.

'But he's no wantin tae leave me empty handed, keeps telling me I'm a cool dude and aw this. Ken what he gave me?'

Michael shook his head.

'A packet eh strawberry Hubba Bubba bubblegum,' Craigy said. 'Can ye believe that? Bloody Hubba Bubba bubblegum. Before he gets oot, he goes, "Get yer gums roond that, my man. Best flavour ae the lot!"'

Michael laughed and felt his phone buzz in his pocket. A new job.

'I better head off, Craigy,' he said, gesturing to his mobile.

'No bother, bud,' Craigy said. 'I'll catch ye after.'

Michael nodded and got back into his cab. Before he pulled away, he reached into the glove box for his notepad and pen. Checking Craigy was out of sight, he scribbled: *Hubba Bubba Bubblegum. Get yer gums roond that, my man.*

Even though he wasn't clocking off until six in the morning, Michael decided he'd write that one up as soon as he got home. He'd make a book out of taxi stories yet.

THE RUTS
James McCulloch

The year was 1979 and it was November. Me and my auld pal Stevie were standing trying to look cool at the Kinema Ballroom in Dunfermline. Who walks up to the bar? Only Malcolm Owen and Segs from The Ruts. They were playing that night, supported by The Flys.

Stevie being Stevie asked Segs what he was drinking. Segs replied, "Tequila. Would you guys like one?" You can guess the answer to that one. Small talk followed then I asked Malcolm if he would sign his autograph on the only piece of paper I had with me, my birth certificate. Yes, this little piece of paper was my back up all those years ago enabling me to enter premises I was legally allowed to frequent anyway.

It was a great night. At one point the band played each other's instruments and still sounded amazing. Great night. Great memories. Sadly missed to the music world.

RIP Malcolm Owen.

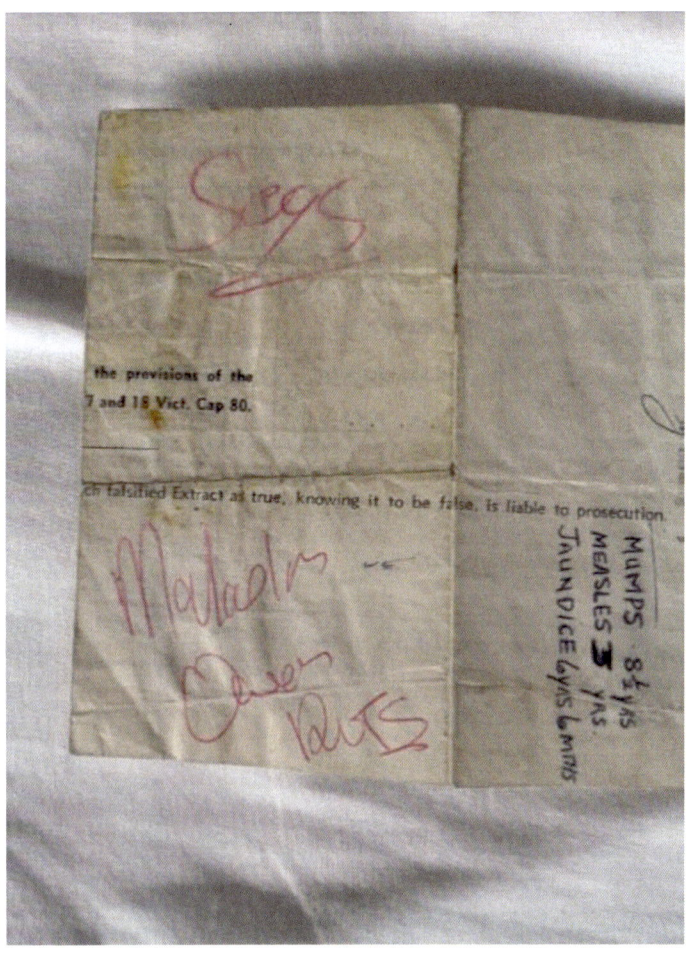

James McCulloch

Tam Main

Scott T. Steel

Gus Rae

FIND YOUR TRIBE
Johnny Da Silva

'Don't
  you
    know
      that
        there's
         a
           door
            to
              the
                here
                  and
                    now?'

Sky was a crystal clear kindest blue
The aureate cut light all shining through
With the sea breeze swaying to and fro
My baby told me 'hey, take it real slow'

And me I had a bird's eye view
It cleansed me, refreshed me, inspired me anew
Even painted my heart
in a technicolour hue

Surround me with Love
let the others pass through
Baby, please stay a while
I promise I'll be true

For I believe in angels
and blood red moons
I seek a life of Spirit
and the Goddess' boons

I'm 90% water,
And ten per cent truth
Now I drink from the fountain
Where I once squandered my youth

The tides near turned me crazy
when l went looking for my tribe
Can I tell you a secret?
Do you want to know mine?

Surround me with Love
let the others pass through
Baby, please stay a while
I promise I'll be true

For I believe in angels
and blood red moons
I need a life of Spirit
and the Goddess' boons

When I was tongue-tied and restless
and soaked thru with brine
My heart never stopped searching
the Chorus Divine

I yearned for serenity
The calm, the calm
The ineffable, the mysterious
Eternal soul balm

I'm along for the ride now
No rushing nor haste
Just the swell of life's tide
and the curves of your grace

Activate and navigate,
transform the world
You – the Light Bringer
The Soul Song – the Soul Singer

Surround me with Love
let the others pass thru
Baby, please stay a while,
I promise I'll be true

For I believe in angels
and blood red moons
I lit the fire of Spirit
through the Goddess' boons

'These
    great
        loves
            are
                for
                    the
                        brave
                            my
                                darling…'

GAMBLING
Janet Crawford

Scabby, discarded and broken
left sitting offset on the pavement
its shine as cracked and broken
as its weary bling dots
Rolled a six again,
ye ken yer doon on yer luck
when ye look oan and curse . . .
As the snake says '*when?*'
Then moves, so ye can sidle past
tae the ladder awaiting yer descent
wi hand grips that fit ye
like gloves knitted that day
Ye'd hae argued the toss
bit whit's the point
when yuv lost at cards
and yer horse huz long bolted
So doon the ladder ye slide
doon and doon till yer
back whaur ye started
oan rung number one

and no a fuckin ladder in sight.

Sometimes looking doon
gies ye a start oan something
that's oan the up . . .

If only ye can grasp that first rung.

Razur Cuts interviews
SONS OF SOUTHERN ULSTER (JUSTIN KELLY & DAVID MEAGHER)

We caught up with Justin Kelly (JK) and David Meagher (DM) in April 2021 to ask them a few questions.

RC: **You hail from Cavan, in Ireland. Tell us a bit about Cavan.**

JK: Cavan is in Ulster, but south of the border. The town we grew up in, Bailieborough, is what's called a planters' town, built mainly by Scottish Presbyterians. Traditionally, this part of Ulster was underserved and by the 70s and early 80s, when we were growing up, there were few amenities. The main industry was farming and there were some factories in the town, so it was a bit of a boom time before the great recession that came later.

As youngsters we'd hang around the town day and night. We'd play pool in the pubs and before long we'd be sneaking in a few pints. Drink was a big part of the culture and while the town only had about 1,500 inhabitants, there were 32 pubs!

While we could see what was going on in Britain with the whole punk scene through the BBC and the NME, we were far removed from that world. Country and western and the showband scene were where it was at back then.

To the powers that be, Cavan people were derided as being a bit thick and were known for being mean and frugal, not unlike the way certain English comedians used to speak of the Scottish. In the mid-80s, David and I spent a summer working in Anstruther in Fife and, I must say, the outlook was very similar to what we'd grown up with: a dour, understated sense of humour and a healthy distrust of authority – and the English. I remember people would try to start fights with us because we were "outsiders". It was just like home really!

DM: Farming, football and fabulous music. It's got its own quirky identity with straight talking folk who have a dry sense of humour.

RC: **When you started playing together in the 80s, how far did it get before real life got in the way? Were you gigging? Did the band have a name?**

JK: We started a band around 1986 called The Panic Merchants, who performed on and off in various guises until about 1992. We mostly played in Dublin in the usual haunts that many now consider legendary: The Underground, The Rock Garden and The Baggot Inn. Apparently, Dublin was swarming with A&R men looking for the next U2 but they kept well away from us! We were enthusiastic but probably a bit derivative. In the end, the band just petered out. We were getting older and I think we'd hit a creative wall. Not sure if we officially broke up. I think we stopped playing gigs for a while and one day I went to the States. It was quite common back then to just up and leave with a couple of hundred quid in your pocket and never come back.

RC: **What prompted you to get back together after a 25-year hiatus?**

JK: After I left Ireland, David and I kept in fairly regular contact. We'd always talk about bands and records and there was a sense there was some unfinished business. My mother died in 2009 and I met up with David and former Panic Merchants' drummer, Noel, at the funeral. We ended up getting together and playing a few of our 'hits' with me on bass. We played a barebones version of 'Love of Jesus' that night, and that started the process of putting together the first album, *Foundry Folk Songs*, but it was a slow process. It didn't appear until 2015, or maybe 2016 – I can't really remember when it came out! When we finally had the album, we had to do a few gigs so we reached out to our original bass player, Paddy. We didn't realise at the time he was living in Australia but he was up for it and the rest, as they say, is history.

DM: For me, I think the notion of the band had been done and dusted for many years until the early noughties and, to be honest, my relationship with music had withered. But then when I came back to Ireland after spells working in Scotland and New Zealand, I started going to a few gigs, mostly local folk stuff like John Spillane. I began to feel that maybe I had, up to that point, really only embraced a narrow enough seam of music with punk and new wave. I started to relearn guitar from a different and more technical angle and thinking about the purpose of music as an expression of life rather than youthful angst.

To be honest, I realised how much brilliant music I had missed first time round and how much I missed music as a core part of my life. I guess then we all hit that phase of life when you have to deal with complicated stuff like responsibility and loss, so you have to dig deeper, and that's where music takes on a different role. That saying, "rock n roll saved my life" suddenly had a lot more meaning!

RC: **If you all had the chance, which musician, if any, would you have play on a track or two?**

JK: The first single I ever bought was 'Like Clockwork' by The Boomtown Rats. I would have been about 12 or 13 and was obsessed with The Rats. At that time, it was unusual for an Irish band to make it big internationally, but what was even more remarkable about them was that the bass player was from Cavan – just up the road a few miles in Ballyjamesduff! This just wasn't our world, as these guys were like mythical creatures.

Step forward 40 or more years and word comes through the grapevine that Pete Briquette has heard our album and not only loves it, but wants to remix a few songs! The stuff of dreams. So now we have an EP of remixes with Pete Briquette – and if you listen to the remix of 'Polaris', I believe Pete has added a bit of bass! So my answer is Pete Briquette.

DM: God, there are so many that come to mind but Davey Ray Moor of CousteauX stands out as a truly brilliant musician and producer. I've started learning the trumpet, so maybe we'll hear a bit of that on the next album.

RC: **Are there any other Irish bands you love, or possibly even aspire to be like?**

DM: Jaysus, this could start a civil war in the band and make us loads of enemies outside it! I think Irish bands suffer from the curse of being a bit too musical, which may seem an odd thing to say, but there is a tendency to have to establish your musical credentials and then push the underlying artistic thing.

For The Sons, we've tried to ditch that approach to things, start with the narrative and let the music follow. I guess bands like The Virgin Prunes, Nun Attax, Sultans of Ping F.C. and Jinx Lennon stand out as having done their own thing brilliantly. Just now there is a greater confidence in the crop of new Irish bands to experiment and find their own sound, and there is a movement of post-punk acts that are really good, but if I start listing names it'll only lead to trouble.

RC: **Album artwork is a major part of a release. How long did it take for the cover art of your latest album *Sinners and Lost Souls* to be finalised? And who does your artwork?**

DM: Along the way we came into contact with Claus Castenskiold, who did the fantastic art for those early Fall albums and *Mother Juno* by The Gun Club, two bands who are historically important to the psyche of The Sons. We got to chatting about our stuff and he liked the concept, so he ended up doing the art for *Sinners and Lost Souls*, the *Turf Accountant Schemes* EP, and a narrative-based textbook on mental illness I did as part of my other job as a psychiatrist. We are delighted with the collaboration as he nails down the cranky nature of what we do.

RC: **How does the writing process work with Justin in the States and the rest of the band in Ireland?**

JK: Basically, we record everything remotely and clean it up later. What's nice about this is you can really take your time and experiment. I don't know if The Sons would work as a full-time band in the conventional sense as when you get to our age, you can become quite cranky and I suspect we would probably fall out. Even on some of our short tours, tempers have been strained! As they say, absence makes the heart grow fonder and I think in a band sense this is very true.

The technology today allows you to be more in control of your music. Years ago, you'd have to record in a professional recording studio and hire an engineer who was invariably a bitter failed musician who'd spend three hours sound checking the drums while you watched the clock because you were paying by the hour. If there were mistakes, you just had to live them. I hated that scene.

DM: It may sound strange, but writing songs whilst apart actually adds to the depth of thought that goes into them. I think when you put stuff together in the melting pot of a rehearsal room, you can sometimes get a bit lazy and let the energy of the noise carry things. But through necessity, we have to listen very closely to where each other is coming from and I think that brings a more coherent product. Ultimately, we come together to record the final takes, so it works well.

Also, as we only get to rehearse and gig twice a year or so, we tend to really use the time efficiently and prepare well for it. I think quite a few bands lose their mojo by spending too much time stuck in rehearsals with each other and that can lead to feuding. We don't have time for any of that – it's all love when The Sons gather!

RC: **What are your rules on bevvying before taking to the stage?**

JK: When we started playing gigs with our first band, we would show up drunk and come off the stage thinking we were brilliant. After listening back to a few tapes, we realised this wasn't the case and brought in a band rule that you could have three pints before a gig. This resulted in certain members, including me, having five or six pints on the way before showing up at the venue for the allotted three pints. I remember many times wanting to vomit halfway through the first song. Nowadays, we're a bit more mature and don't drink before a gig. We just have 20 pints after!

RC: **Favourite toilet paper?**

JK: I'm glad you asked! I'm very much a fan of the industrial type – cheap and strong. It probably stems from my schooldays when we used to have square sheets of greaseproof paper that took some getting used to, but made me who I am. I can't stand cushioned, quilted, or – worst of all – perfumed, and feel that if you're using them, you may as well be wiping your arse with a towel, or the curtains.

My preference may, or may not, explain the lyric – "that leave the arse red raw and a man on his knees begging for his maker to take him this very minute".

DM: Superabsorbent with aloe vera. Life teaches you never to skimp on beds, shoes, guitars and bog roll! We deserve the best that money can buy for these essentials.

RC: **Hindsight is a wonderful thing. Looking back, would you have done anything differently?**

JK: Musically, no. I'm very happy with what we are doing and the pace at which we work. Personally, I would have done a lot differently – I'd have been kinder and more forgiving of people, and myself.

DM: In the old days, I think we should have invested in better gear, gigged less, recorded more and not boozed before gigs! With The Sons, I think we are more patient and thoughtful about what we're doing, the message we're communicating and how it'll stand the test of time. It would be nice to gig more, but it's tough being so dispersed across the globe.

RC: **Which artist or artists do you listen to to relax?**

JK: I find myself listening to a lot of Cocteau Twins lately. Over the years, I've gone back and forth with them. At times I've thought they were a bit pretentious, but when they hit the heights, they truly soar. And the Velvet Underground. And Neil Young. I guess I'm becoming a hippie, but you can't listen to Anti-Nowhere League all the time.

DM: Friday evening starts with the Mickey Bradley show on BBC Radio Ulster and then later on gets a bit more mellow with the likes of Richmond Fontaine, Sparklehorse, Feist, Orange Juice and maybe a bit of John Cooper Clarke to spice it up!

THE GIRL WITH GREEN HAIR
Stuart McIntosh

My indestructible girl.
You lie broken, yet calmly resilient and awake
within these whitewashed walls.

I hear nothing but silence.

My iridescent girl.
Your painted nails clash with the blood that clings
to your fingers and stings my eyes.

I see nothing but strength.

My empathy girl.
Trapped behind white-knuckle handrails
and needles that seem to hold your entire face together.

I feel nothing but fear.

My semi-permanent girl.
Your dyed green hair is matted in warm wet patches
and you ask if I'm okay, through the pain of your
adversity.

I remember nothing but love.

My inexorable girl.

You look up at me as if personifying existence itself, emanating from under a single strand of luminescent hair.

I sense nothing but fire.

My incandescent girl.
Flesh and bone bound to steel, as a morphine racked stream of words that, unfiltered and unflustered, dance between anger and joy.

I taste nothing but the fight.

Nobody can take my girl with green hair away.
Not death, or the end of the world.

OLD FAGS
Will B

Woodbine and Capstan
Paper wrapped in five
Unfiltered lung terrorists
Of days gone by

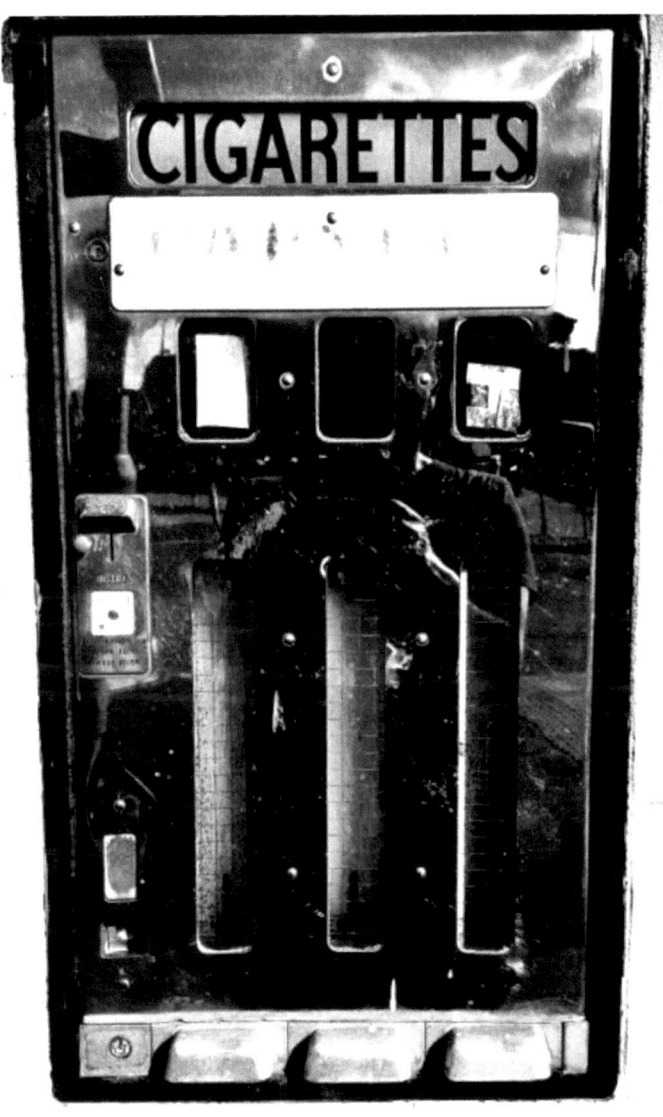

Will B

Derek S

Derek S

Tam Main

Razur Cuts interviews
JB BARRINGTON

We first saw Salford-based JB Barrington supporting Sleaford Mods in Edinburgh in 2015. Performing poetry to that kind of crowd was never going to be easy, but he slayed them with his quick-witted, working class prose. His book *Woodchip Anaglypta & Nicotined Artex Ceilings* comes highly recommended. We caught up with JB in November 2016 for a chat.

RC: **Where was your first gig and can you remember it?**

JB: 1978, 11th floor of Canon Hussey Court, Salford; me gran and grandad's flat. My dad asked me to do my Rigsby impression for their neighbour, Mrs Potts, which went down a storm. Everything else just pales into insignificance, ha ha!

First gig, er, well, I did loads of stuff before the poetry lark, which incidentally I fell into by accident. I used to write raps as I was proper into hip hop and did some live stuff at a club called City Lites in Bolton back in 1988/89. I also used to play guitar and write songs – still do – but weren't any good at singing an that, so first poetry gig was at Paul Heaton's pub, The Kings Arms in Salford. Paul held a poetry night called *Poems and Pints* and it was March 2012. He knew I was writing songs, playing guitar an that, so he asked me to do some of my songs as poems at his night, so I did. It was a

Friday and Mike Garry, Gav Roberts and some other poets were on the bill. That was the start of it all I suppose.

The night was compered by a guy called Mike O'Brien who used to be in a Hull band called Mike Montez & The Velvetones, which I was a huge fan of from the John Peel days – so that coupled with the fact Paul Heaton had asked me to perform *and* was in the audience made it all the more special.

RC: **Were you always into poetry or did you write stories too? Were you in a band at any time?**

JB: I always loved song lyrics. The first realisation of this was getting a copy of The Jam's *Setting Sons* for Christmas 1979 off our kid. The lyrics in 'Little Boy Soldiers' and 'Private Hell' really resonated with me – they related to my mam's world, my gran's world and the world of everyone on our estate. Those words meant everything to me, so much more than anything I was being taught at school. Was I in a band? Yes, several, but they were shite, I was shite. I couldn't really sing.

RC: **Do you jot things down as part of your daily routine, or make mental notes?**

JB: I write every day. I constantly put things on bits of paper and/or into a note thingy on my phone. My phone is full of stuff; my notes and ideas are all over the place. It reminds me of that great poster in Travis Bickle's apartment in *Taxi Driver* that says "One of these days I'm gonna get organized". I need to get it all sorted.

RC: **Have you ever spontaneously performed a poem in the heat of the moment after witnessing something?**

JB: Yes, 'Sunglasses' is one of em, as is 'The Nauseating Need for Nostalgia'.

RC: **Your first job?**

JB: Proper job? That would have been YTS Plumbing in 1987 and I was also a pot collector in the local labour club to subsidise the £27.50 a week paid by the government. I was a paperboy before that and I also did a bit of window cleaning, covering for our kid when he got sent down, but that's another story.

    The pot collecting job was the best cos that's where all the ideas to write came from: the old dockers, the concert room turns, the committee men; all those that frequented that labour club, absolutely brilliant, comedic geniuses all of em. I remember me and my mate Jason Lightfoot would go round the club collecting glasses, but we'd have to make sure we only took those that were dead[*] – so we'd purposely go up to the old guys, the hardened drinkers, when their pints were full, and say, "Is that dead, mate?" They'd look up and say, "You fuckin will be if you take it".

    I wrote a poem called 'The Vault' all about them times – it's in a now defunct copy of my first book, *Words for Class Heroes,* but I think I might put it in my new book, which will have all of everything I've ever written so far.

---

[*] empty or finished with

RC: **Obvious question now – your influences?**

JB: The ex-Salford dockers in the labour club, the aforementioned concert room turns and committee men, my mam and all her bingo mates, and the neighbours on our estate in Little Hulton. They all had an influence on me, they all made me want to write, they all made me want to record their idiosyncrasies. They fascinated me.

Other influences would deffo be Paul Weller, Paul Heaton, Billy Bragg, Elvis Costello and a guy called Shorn Braithwaite aka MC Buzz B, plus the likes of Chuck D from Public Enemy.

RC: **What did you have for your tea last night?**

JB: Chips, sausage and beans with three rounds of bread and butter.

RC: **Do you have a wee drink to relax before performing?**

JB: Yeah, but I don't do it to relax. I have a drink because I'm a drunk.

RC: **Who is your current favourite poet and who should we look out for?**

JB: Marvin Cheeseman. He's everything you need to know about poetry.

RC: **Is it cheesy toast, toasted cheese or roasted cheese?**

JB: None of them, it's cheese on toast. There's toast and if you put some cheese on it, the cheese is on the toast, so . . . you get cheese on toast.

RC: **It's all too common to see a performer on stage and a talking crowd in front of them. How do you deal with that situation?**

JB: Easy, just be louder. As Bernard Manning always said, "I've got the microphone." I think if I walked out and did 'I wandered lonely as a cloud' type poems then maybe I'd have a problem, but I don't – I hit em hard and fast and get right into it, then I take em up and down, and then, if I do get some noise, I just tell em to shut the fuck up . . . but it dunt really happen too often. I do get the odd heckle, which is cool, but I just nail em. I've got the microphone.

I had a shithead once shout "John Cooper Clarke impressionist!" I just shouted back, "Fuck off mate, first of all that's a compliment and secondly, you should see me do Mike Yarwood". I had another heckle whilst supporting Sleaford Mods in Leeds where this woman was offended because I'd used the word cunt. She was going on about how the word was misogynistic to women. Now bear in mind my missus is a feminist and our house is festooned with Suffragettes memorabilia. I just shouted back "Sorry, but I cunt hear you, I cunt see you and I cunt tell what you were saying". Then Sleaford Mods came on and opened up with their track, 'Bunch of Cunts'. Oh the irony, you *cunt* make it up.

RC: **We heard your mum stopped you being a punk! Did you like punk because of the lyrical content in the songs?**

JB: That's mad, how d'ya know that? It was actually my dad. I weren't really a punk, but I kinda tried. I remember meticulously trying to copy the exact font from *The Great Rock 'n' Roll Swindle* album in marker on the back of a C&A jacket and my mam would pass it over the garden wall cos my dad had told her to put it in the bin.

See, I came to it all late, around 1979/80, cos you gotta remember at the height of what was real punk, circa 1977, I was only six. Later on though, as an eight or nine-year-old, I met a lad on our estate called Howard Beaumont, who I pay homage to in my poem 'First of The Ninth'. I was walking down Longshaw Drive in Little Hulton and he shouted from his bedroom window to come in, so I went in and he played me 'Friggin in the Riggin' by The Sex Pistols on his mam's radiogram, which was the B-side of the Sid Vicious single, 'Something Else'. Well, I was hooked; I wanted some of that.

Then I met Robert Taylor, a cool guy on our estate with a great record collection, who I'm still mates with today. He put me onto Stiff Little Fingers and The Clash. What was the question again? Oh yeah, lyrical content. Well, The Clash certainly did that, as did Stiff Little Fingers – 'Spanish Bombs' is still one of my favourite songs, as is 'Alternative Ulster', but at that time I was more attracted to the mod revival thing, although I didn't know it was a revival at the time.

GORDON
THE TRAFFIC WARDEN
JB Barrington

My mate Gordon the traffic warden
Fired fines from machine stroke Gatling gun
He was starkly officious hardly auspicious
Fly postering windscreens with tickets for fun

He was bereft of any compassion
He was duty bound to browbeat
You'd think he'd been born in that uniform
As he goose stepped down the high street

Absolutely autocratic and always ecstatic
When a tyre was touching two yellow lines
And with a grin above chin whilst dribbling
He'd do a foxtrot whilst flinging our fines

My mate Gordon the traffic warden
Was vile, volatile and venomous
Taking pictures daily thinking he's David Bailey
Snapping offending cars for evidence

Through the churches litany he had an epiphany
He knelt at the altar and drank from the font
Then my mate Gordon the traffic warden
Heard God say let em all park where they want

After seeing the light he let em park where they like
The tickets and fines were no more
My mate Gordon the traffic warden
The shopkeepers and shoppers did truly adore

The sign on the bay 30 minutes did say
But the lady overstayed by two hours
She was illegally parked but he didn't get narked
He just gave her a kiss and a bouquet of flowers

The local authority all voted by a majority
To have Gordon the traffic warden taken away
And now if you wanna see him he's in Salford museum
They've stuffed him and put him on display

SELF-DESTRUCTION II: DREAMS TAKE MY FIGHT
Kirsty Allison

There's a time when I'm the crease on the bag
The hole in the rubbish sack
Queen of slack
The live forever plastic flag
In the disappointing breeze of the tree

I'm the Deliveroo driver who can't stand and deliver
your rider at the gig with a PhD viva,
I forget your cider
I am cancer
The warmth you mither, I'm no river
I am dried out milk
Lost turkeyneck strands of silk
Broken glass on a guilt quilt
Chastity beneath kilt
It's not your fault
I'm salt in a burial vault
Rhizomatic automatic
Future attics
I am lager not ale
Post wedding-veil
the piss on the rim
The grey prism
The shit on the shoe

The question mark stew
I am no Joan of Arc
These wages are frail, I am the nail
In your coffin, and only death will change this
Red blacklist
Taped to the right of the double glaze of the screen
Dug from my vein
From the glint of the hat pin you gave me through this
two-way mirror,
Shrill terrier yapping night terror
I'm at the post box, sending bait
Old bean eyes flash down the grate
You mistake my scum laude light in the tunnel
Coming towards you, down the thief gunnel
As a love letter
voodooed as a debtor
Away from this island of stolen land
dead people piling up at the door
Diversions cannoning fodder,
Congestion manoeuvres
Angles pointing at stripped down councils
Dodgem pounds.
I'm so self-involved
Overexposed, available
Distracted by a lost keyring

The next big thing
Lint strobe
Flashing my bathrobe
Space probe
On the way to therapy
You say my generosity is not narcissity
Vainglorious demonstrous lights of the stage
Cheekbones to the grave

No freedom of whirling in circles
It's just too heterosexual
Level zero, aim higher
fix and mend better
I will never ghost desire
These hauntings will get you
I'm impressed, by your impressions
Influenced by your reception
And I will always love you

THE FALL
Julian Colton

In Memoriam
Mark E. Smith
(not that he would want it)

Mancunian contrariness abounds
A steadfast refusal to playlist the old songs
High rise, terraced housing slum clearance prodigy

Eclectic mix of 50s baby boomery
An Alex Harvey, Captain Beefheart self-moulded deity –
Bowie, Ferry, Brecht and Brel, even Elvis and Rodgers & Hart

I imagine a scissored-from-the-same-cloth beginning:
Hanging out by the Underground Market and Kippax Street
Robbing LPs from Rare Records and HMV

Sneaking into flea-pit *Cabaret* and *A Clockwork Orange*
Knowing what you want and who you are
From the Sex Pistols Free Trade Hall start

Ending each flat sprung lyric line with an 'Ah'
An off-key autodidact soundtrack to youth

Totally Wired
      The North Will Rise Again
            Spoilt Victorian Child

Despite Michael Clark prancing around in his bare arse
How many students and *Guardian* readers
Could tolerate, stomach you in real life?

Band members removed like rotten milk teeth
A form of addiction – losing friends and lovers
Quicker than cut-off electricity

An outsider as Kafka, Sartre and Camus
Looking like a grandad before your time
Northern social, pub and club parody

Exploded star fixed to disintegrate trajectory
Uncompromising, your art takes its toll
The premature death of you, amphetamines and alcohol

The Beats and Joplin, Hendrix, Byron, Blake and Morrison
Knew more comes from living it, total immersion
But the road of excess leads to demise as well as the Palace of Wisdom.

You must have been trying to impress someone
A mother, a father figure, a teacher, a woman?
Yourself? You can't thrive in a self-sealed vacuum

Not everyone will love you now you are gone
Those who closed their eyes and hoped you'd die when alive
Will come out of the woodwork to take a kick at you.

Some might prefer to faintly praise you
This nation's saving graces, there are but few.

KNAVISH TRICKS TO CRUSH
John Tinney

Lizzie 2's crown slid off as she took to the floor for the first time in a decade and looked under Andrew's bed. *Why is this insubordinate ingrate cutting up perfectly good clothes and sticking safety pins through them? What more psychological defects can this boy inherit from his father?*

The Clash, The Ramones, The Sex Pistols? A bag of grass and a packet of off-white residue lay inside the sleeve for *Never Mind the Bollocks*. Lizzie 2 tasted the speed like a seasoned drug trafficker. *Drugs! As if it wasn't bad enough with his tantrums, nature and that accent he's adopted, now he's graduated to drugs and these grubby records.*

It was pure morbid curiosity, but she looked again at her defacement and shuddered as guitars and drums assaulted her sophisticated ears. *Why are such derogatory remarks about me the stuff of pop culture? If I'm not a human being, what the hell am I? A giraffe. Fascist? Those Nazi salute photos must never see the light of day.* She hated to admit it, but it was quite catchy. Her foot tapped away, and she hummed the tune as she pulled out a box full of safety pins. *He's obviously been using these to pierce holes in the tin foil on this plastic bottle. Definite drug paraphernalia.* Andy saw the lock on his door was broken and burst into his room to find his mother sitting on his bed, listening to his illicit stash of records.

'You broke intae ma room?'

'I told you I would get Jeeves to remove the lock if that smell continued to emanate from your room. And stop speaking in that ridiculous accent, Andrew.'

'Whit ridiculous accent?'

'You're not a Glaswegian chimney sweep.'

'Chimney sweep? Whit is this, *Oliver Twist*? It's 1978. You need tae get in touch wae reality.'

'Says the upper-class English boy, who thinks he can become working class and Glaswegian on a rebellious whim after listening to that hairy comedian he saw on *Parkinson*.'

'Don't you oppress me! Ah can speak any wey Ah bloody well want!'

'No, you can't. You're a prince . . . of sorts.'

Andrew's face contorted like he'd caught a whiff of sewage. 'Aw this egregious wealth, elevated status and pageantry . . .'

'Yes, what of it?'

'It's archaic and morally bankrupt.'

'Oh! And I suppose you want to go to work in a factory for eight hours a day and live in a council flat? I could arrange that.'

'Eh . . .'

'You can lose all your privilege and I can set you up in a job and flat in Glasgow. I'm sure you'll fit in with that accent.'

'Ah'm only 14.'

'When the time comes . . .'

'Ah'll dae it maself. Naebody ever does anything for themselves in this family.'

'Sure you will, but, firstly, you can take down that poster.'

'That's art. And it's ma right tae self-expression.'

Lizzie 2 sighed. 'Son, if you're trying to hurt me, you

need not bother. I'm not human. I'm just like those Pistol boys say. And they've got another thing right. There is no democracy in this palace. This is a dictatorship, and I'm the dictator. Now, stop cutting up your clothes and sticking safety pins through them. You're not a poor kid with no other choice, and for that you should be eternally grateful.'

Andy took down the poster and made a scene about it. Lizzy 2 finally left the room to tell someone to tell the chef to prepare the munchies. Andy looked at Travis Bickle on the wall and his latest epiphany hit him like a size 15 boot smacking a football through a window.

The whole table was aghast at the vision of horror that interrupted dinner. Blood trickled from the safety pin punctured through Andy's left ear, and his Mohawk made Phillip even more incomprehensible and incandescent with rage. The Queen squirmed in her luxurious seat. There were more than a few questions, but Andy just mimed putting a gun to his head and repeatedly pulling the trigger.

URINAL CAKE
Chris McQueer

Gary stared down at his steady flow of pish. The music was quieter in the toilet and his ears were ringing after being pummelled by the pounding bass for hours. This was his first pee of the night and he'd sunk five pints – it was a big, powerful belter. He pointed the stream directly onto the urinal cake and smiled as wee bits started to break off the yellow cube.

Pick it up and eat it, the voice in his head said.

He wasn't schizophrenic or anything like that. Just every now and again his brain would try to make him do something weird.

Sometimes it happened when he went for a haircut. Gary had long hair down to his shoulders. He'd sit down in the chair and the barber would ask what he wanted. Instead of replying with "Just the usual, cheers" (an inch taken off every six weeks), he'd feel compelled to blurt out, "Gies a baldy!" He'd managed to avoid that happening so far.

Then there was the time in the gym. The wee voice said he should probably pick up a 20kg weight plate and throw it like a Frisbee across the gym. Just to see what would happen.

When he worked in McDonald's, he came very close to plunging his hand into the chip fryer. He had to quit after that.

Pick it up and eat it, the voice said again. There was a guy standing next to him. Gary's pee ended abruptly. The guy next to him was still going strong. He was going to have to wait until the guy was finished so he could eat the urinal cake.

He glanced over once again to see if the guy was close to finishing. Finally, he gave his dick a shake and tucked it back into his denims. Gary breathed a sigh of relief. He put his own penis away and followed the guy over to the sink. All he had to do now was take longer to wash his hands and he could satisfy his urge. No-one would see him eating the urinal cake and he could enjoy the rest of his night.

Gary looked in the mirror, still washing his hands. The guy was drying his hands and staring at him. Gary stopped and joined him at the hand dryer. He gave the guy a wee smile. The guy gave up drying his hands and wiped them on his denims, clearly in a hurry to get out of the toilet and away from Gary.

THE PUB BORE'S STALE TALE
Bobby Gant

The last one I told didn't react too badly. Bought me another pint afterwards so he did. Thought it was a bad idea for a film but felt for me. Said nobody deserves to lose their job due to a bad idea. He's right as well, isn't he? Put on trial and found guilty for having a bad idea. This is the free world, for Christ's sake.

I do this every day now and in some respects I've never been happier. Half a stout and regular shots of brandy, perched at this corner of the bar like a fixture or fitting, like part of the furniture they say. And every day without fail, I engage somebody, initially in your regular tedious pub conversation but then I tell them my story. I tell them I used to have a career as a scriptwriter and I used to pitch ideas for films to some of the London studios, even occasionally over in L.A. They look sceptical at first but then I tell them that I lost my job and things fall into place – it starts to seem believable.

Nobody believes the pub bore – the pub philosopher – has a career or even ever did anything other than drink in the exact same spot. Nobody believes it until you tell them you've lost your job and then it becomes believable. They latch on to the sense of tragedy. And by telling them this story, by telling a different person every day about my film idea, the infamous idea that changed my life . . . by doing that, I bring it to life. That film is more real now than it would be even if it was on the big screen in a Leicester Square cinema. How about that?

The last one took it quite well. I told him the details. It starts with this main character called Liam and the funny thing is he thinks he's some kind of Liam Gallagher type chancer. Get it? The only thing worse than actually being Liam Gallagher is wanting to be him. That's too pathetic for words. So the opening scene more or less is Liam having a threesome with two young girls. Legal though, but only just. One is based on Greta Thunberg, called Gretchen. The other is based on Millie Bobby Brown, called Milana. Tongues in arseholes, the whole works but like a bad dream, you know? Like it shouldn't be happening, which I guess it shouldn't, but it's a free world, isn't it? Supposed to be.

When he's finished up there (nothing graphic), he goes down into this garden that is sort of exotic. You can hear all these exotic birds and jungle animals and the grass is more vivid than in this country; a neon green grass. And he gets in this rowing boat at the bottom of the garden and floats away down this river. Now, that sounds strange but stranger still is this goes on for ages – time becomes meaningless to him. One river joins another river joins another river.

I'm telling this stranger all of this and he's just listening and sipping his pint and nodding his head.

So one river becomes another and Liam starts talking to beavers and herons and fish and shit like that. Real dark one-way conversations because ultimately he regrets something, like all men, and eventually this river changes again and it becomes the sea.

On the sea he just bobs around in this boat and his hair and beard grow out like Tom Hanks in *Castaway*, which was a good movie by the way cos it takes skill to write a movie with only one character in it for a long time. Bobbing around on this vast grey ocean where you can't tell where the water ends and the sky begins and he starts talking to God, right? Not in an extreme way and not asking for help, just talking to him about his life and the things he's done and seen and experienced. And you never know how God has taken it, but there is a huge, desperate storm and it sends Liam overboard, sinking his little boat for good. So, essentially he drowns.

While I'm telling all this, the man just keeps nodding away, drinking his pint real nonchalantly and I have a certain respect for that, let me tell you.

So, Liam drowns and then something really weird happens, but this is cinema. Strange things happen all the time. Look at *Eraserhead* for crying out loud!

When I shout, the man doesn't react, just drinks his pint and again I think *respect*.

Something weird happens. Liam becomes a kind of sea creature, almost like a mermaid but not female. And then nothing really happens until Gretchen is crossing the Atlantic on a boat like she sometimes does and she comes across Mermaid Liam and shoots the poor bastard with a harpoon, right through the arch between his shoulder blades. He's killed instantly and Gretchen just drags him behind the boat all the way to America – very cold and very casual attitude to it all, that's important in the film, how calm she is.

As she's dragging this corpse through the murky water, gulls and sharks and fish are taking chunks out of him. Eating him basically, as is nature's way. When the boat reaches America, all that's left is the top section of the spine and the skull, completely devoid of flesh or hair or anything. Clean as a whistle.

The last scene has Milana and Gretchen back together. They're sat on a beach, a completely empty beach. It isn't a nice day, quite windy and overcast. Again, that's important. The two of them are building a sandcastle and the final scene has them erecting the spine and skull out of the top of the sandcastle like a flag. Then the film ends, the scene just sort of fades into a misty darkness and all you can hear is the wind and the waves in the distance. Reminds you of that Polanski film, *Cul-de-sac*, sort of.

I got sacked for that. Can you believe it? Still think it would have been a hell of a film. The last one, he didn't agree but he was sorry I'd lost my job. You could see that – genuine sympathy but he wasn't patronising about it. Bought me a pint. Said nobody deserves to lose their job because of a bad idea.

'You're right,' I said, 'you're right.'

Razur Cuts interviews
JON ZIP McNEILL (THE ZIPS)

The Zips were formed in Glasgow in 1977 and are still writing and performing today. We met Jon Zip McNeill (JM) one Saturday afternoon in Glasgow in March 2019 to have a blether about The Zips' career, which spans more than four decades.

RC: **What were your humble beginnings, where did you meet, and was music played in your home from an early age?**

JM: My dad was from Islay, so there were a lot of Gaelic connections. My Grandma would take me to Ceilidhs as a youngster where I'd be encouraged to get up and sing. I'd also listen to Beatles songs, subconsciously trying to add another verse. This, in a way, was me introducing myself to song writing. At school, I won a Burns Federation award and I was always interested in poetry and English literature, also enjoying Shakespeare.

I started writing basic songs in the 70s and I met Brian Jackson, a guitarist. We practised in a cupboard in my flat to stifle the noise, as the old woman upstairs would bang her brush on the floor if we became too loud. The cupboard stank of cat piss as the previous tenant was an elderly lady who owned many cats, and the cupboard was where they lived!

I was also in an amateur dramatic company called The Apollo Players. We'd do *West Side Story* and *Sweet Charity* in old people's homes. That was my first foray into playing live.

Once we got a band together, we called ourselves Road Angel and got gigs in pubs and clubs playing covers but adding in a few of our own songs as time went on. We were basically a pub rock band like Joe Strummer's original band, The 101ers. We had a residency at the Acurious Lounge, Glasgow, where we kept our gear. We were once asked to play upstairs to a deaf audience as the band booked for that event had to cancel late. That audience were extremely appreciative as they could feel the vibration of the drums and bass. Our bass player, Phil Mullen, loved it as he could crank up the volume to max!

At weekends, we headed off to play village halls. We were playing on the same bill as Slik and Dead End Kids at that time. Punk records still hadn't been released, we'd only read about it in the papers, and there was no internet in these days of course. It was 1977 and I couldn't wait to buy this new music I was desperate to be a part of. When I eventually heard it, it reminded me of the early energy of The Rolling Stones, The Who and The Small Faces. I had to be involved in it.

My band members weren't keen and we split up, but Brian contacted me a few months later to say he'd heard more punk music that he enjoyed – so we were back together, adding Joe Jaconelli on drums. We then became The Zips, writing new songs and advertising for gigs in McCormack's music shop. You have to remember, in Glasgow at this time, as with other cities, punk rock was banned. Establishments wouldn't put on a punk band for fear of having their license revoked. This is why The Bungalow in Paisley became so prevalent at that time. Bands got to play there.

However, our first gig as The Zips was in March 1978 in Drumchapel. The current line-up of The Zips is the longest running line-up we've had. This has been since 2010. The line-up is Jon Zip, Phil Volume, Fred X and Buddy Poor.

RC: **What was The Zips' first release?**

JM: Our first release was called *The Zips EP*, subsidised by a chap called CJ 'Hannibal' Hayes and we had a 500 pressing in 1979.

Bruce's record shop and a place called Tape Exchange stocked them. Everything was done separately in those days. The pressing, the centre labels and the picture sleeves were all done by different companies, so it was quite worrying as you had to hope everything matched up and at the correct time. The EP sold out in 5 weeks – we were ecstatic. Danny Mac now states that one sold recently for over £400! By this time, John Peel had picked up on it and played every track. This opened us up to a much wider audience. That kudos of having John Peel playing your songs was tremendous.

We then noticed a change in the punk scene as ska was entering into the fray, so our second single, 'Radioactivity', in 1980, was ska influenced. We released 1000 copies and our guitarist Brian's granny financed the whole thing!

Everyone was paid back after the sales had done well as this was what punk was all about – DIY at its very best. That particular single didn't sell too well as the punks weren't keen on it and neither were fans of ska, as they knew us as a punk band. So that went pear-shaped. As songwriters, we didn't want to write the same type of song all the time. We took influences from The Clash and The Ruts, who were also doing reggae songs along with punk. We still sold 600 copies of the single but being left with 400 was disheartening.

RC: **How did the crowds react to you back in the day?**

JM: The Paisley crowd were great because they had been exposed to punk – many bands played in Paisley, so they supported the scene. We were accepted everywhere to be honest; the people understood what we were all about. As the cities had banned punk, places like Falkirk, Paisley and Dunfermline got all the exposure to the top acts. When you think of it, not one Glasgow punk band ever appeared on *Top of the Pops*, but bands like The Rezillos and Skids did. This was because the towns they came from had better exposure to the whole scene.

RC: **The target audience for punk was generally underage, but you got around this. Please tell us about it.**

JM: Yes, this was obvious to the band early on, we were very aware of it. So, I noticed at Custom House Quay on the banks of the Clyde, an amphitheatre, a bandstand with concrete steps for access, really well constructed. There was plastic Perspex all the way around to amplify the sound, so you didn't need a perfect PA. I contacted the council asking to book a pop band and they gave me dates that were available. We got a crowd via word of mouth and promotion from Radio Clyde DJ Brian Ford, who championed the gigs on his show. The booking was a three-hour slot, so we invited other bands to play. One such band was Raw Deal, who were The McCluskey brothers, who then became The Bluebells.

RC: **Our younger readers always ask us about the punk look, so what type of clothing would you be wearing in those days?**

JM: Punks would have spiked hair held up by soap or cola to keep it solid. Straight-legged trousers with baseball boots. To be honest, we didn't really have a fashion sense as punk was about what was in your mind and how you thought – it was an attitude, it wasn't about fashionable clothing. If you look at some Buzzcocks pics from back then, you can see they felt the same in that respect. That said, some punks customised their T-shirts, took their trousers in themselves and made it personal. Again, the DIY approach was adopted. The coloured Mohican-style hairdos with luxury paint jobs on the leather bondage jackets didn't materialise until the 80s punk scene.

RC: **Tell us about 'Death of a Poser'.**

JM: 'Death of a Poser' was a nod to Gary Borland, who sadly passed away in 2018 – he was the lead singer of Heavy Drapes. It was a song I wrote for him after his death. However, I changed the name to 'End of an Era' as I felt the song would be construed in the wrong manner. Tarbeach Records of New York had signed Reaction, a punk band from Airdrie, and when the owner heard of Heavy Drapes and Gary being so vociferous about his band, they simply had to sign them.

I think Gary was the perfect front man, with the attitude that made people say, "Let's go and see Heavy Drapes". I was quite emotional when he passed away because I knew the band and the chemistry they had going. It was sad for that to be taken away from them. The Zips also benefitted from our gigs with them – the scene had been revitalised.

RC: **How did punk affect your family? Also, tell us of the new band you formed called Passionate Friends.**

JM: My parents knew I was in bands, but they didn't know the genres. At the time of punk, I was married and had one daughter – I haven't really asked her if punk had an effect on her. I do have a recording of her singing 'Brass in Pocket' by The Pretenders when she was about two years old though, so she did pick up on some of the songs. I have three brothers but only my youngest brother, Alan, came to the gigs with me. We'd take in gigs by The Stranglers and The Clash at Glasgow Apollo.

After a few lean years, I formed a band in the early 80s with my two brothers, called Passionate Friends. The name was taken from The Teardrop Explodes' song title and we were more of a pop band, but with funk and Echo and the Bunnymen coming through. Each of us had our own thoughts about what we sounded like as there was a lot going on. We had our own label called Tenement Toons and immediately Billy Sloan picked up on our first single 'Time Bandits/What's the Odds' and Radio Clyde gave it overwhelming support.

It was released in March 1983. The lady on the desk at Radio Clyde kindly offered to hand out the single to every A&R person who entered the building and, before we knew it, people were contacting us! I wondered – why didn't this happen with The Zips, as we'd spent long hours travelling to London trying to promote ourselves? Passionate Friends played Night Moves in Glasgow every Sunday evening with Richard Park DJ-ing. We were then signed to MCA who had also signed Kim Wilde and Nik Kershaw. Once those two had hits, all the marketing money went into promoting them. We still got support slots to Rod Stewart, The Police and Big Country. Having Harvey Goldsmith as the promoter was massive for us – we had some great gigs because of him.

When we went to London to sign with MCA, we were told we had a two single, one album deal. However, they changed it to just the singles to minimise the risk. We decided to sign anyway. How could we go home and say we didn't sign? After

The Zips, it was great to have finally signed with a major label but once you're in, you realise you're only on the first rung of the ladder. It's a tough business. We eventually left the label as they changed their minds on the second single, saying they didn't think it would sell. It was released but never promoted. It was the early 80s and for 18 months I found myself unemployed. Looking back though, we did have a great time while it lasted and we met some lovely people.

RC: **Now the obligatory question. Is it cheese on toast, cheesy toast, roasted cheese or toasted cheese?**

JM: I would say cheese on toast, but my wife is from Grangemouth and her dad calls it roasted cheese. So, roasted cheese must be a Central Scotland thing!

RC: **Here's another silly one . . . What was your favourite TV programme from these three?** *The Magic Roundabout, Roobarb & Custard* **or** *Captain Pugwash*?

JM: Oooooh, I actually watched them all, but in my opinion a programme called *The Singing Ringing Tree* was the best; it was a Czechoslovakian programme for kids, but it was very scary. That's the one I've never forgotten. Your readers need to see it!

TRICKS OF THE TRADE
Jared A. Carnie

At this poetry weekend
(don't judge me – it was free)
we were told this clever trick
to allow us to write
about real people
from our real lives
without offending them.

Just tweak the details
they said.

If your brother went to Iraq
and you want to write about it
say your sister went to Iraq.

If you have a difficult relationship
with your dad then write
about a *stepdad* instead.

I didn't think much of the idea.
It doesn't seem particularly helpful
or particularly effective.

In fact, it seems a lot like the inane
inconsequential advice my manager
sometimes gives me.

Sorry, I mean step-manager.

Anne Whyte

Gregor Boyd

Sean Fitzgerald

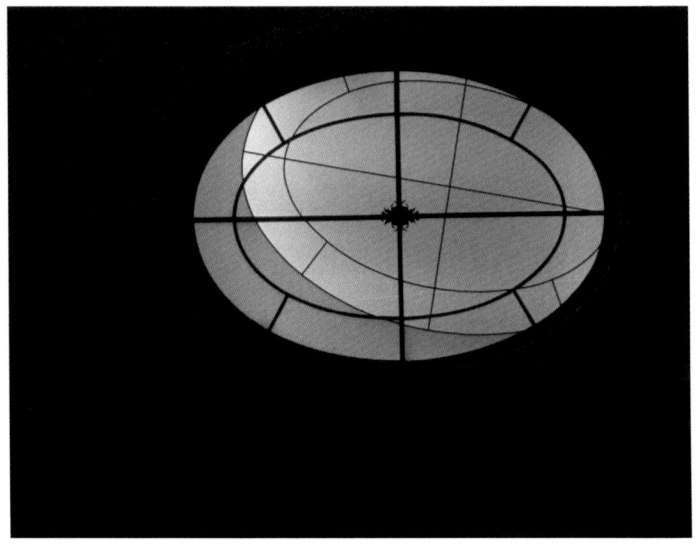

Sean Fitzgerald

Razur Cuts interviews
THE MOONLANDINGZ

We caught up with Adrian (A) from one of the best live acts around, The Moonlandingz, in February 2017.

RC: **Tell us about your self-description of the band – "A semi-fictional Ouija pop group"**

A: The Moonlandingz was born solely from my imagination, from a semi-true story I wrote about a woman stalking the lead singer of a fictional group called The Moonlandingz, in a fictional South Yorkshire ex-mining village called Valhalla Dale.

It was based on my own experience of being stalked by a woman when I was a solo artist of sorts. This became an album for The Eccentronic Research Council, my other project with Dean Honer, my musical partner in The Moonlandingz. The Eccentronic Research Council is a practical analogue electronics and spoken word project that we do with the actress Maxine Peake.

This specific album was called *Johnny Rocket, Narcissist and Music Machine . . . I'm your biggest fan!* To lend the album a bit more depth, Dean and I wrote some music of how I imagined the group sounding – a kind of fuzzy, psychedelic, Joe Meek thing. Then I got Lias and Saul up to Sheffield for a couple of days to contribute some vocals and guitar to the tracks, which was a worthwhile experiment. They then went back to their other band, Fat

White, and Dean and I spent a month or so developing and producing the recordings and getting the tracks sounding like futuristic hits using broken old analogue machines and a dirty old Ouija board . . . and thus, a semi-fictional Ouija pop group was born!

RC: **You've been together a relatively short time and been massively well received. You must be ecstatic about this. Is everything going as planned? We saw you in Glasgow and it was a fuckin riot!**

A: Thank you. Naturally I'm really pleased with how things have been received, but I really did believe that what we had created was – and is – pretty special. There really was no plan though. Once our first single and first ever recording, 'Sweet Saturn Mine' went to radio and was immediately playlisted, followed by a live radio session for Marc Riley that went down really well, it was kind of a no brainer, certainly for Lias, Dean and I, that it was worth pursuing further.

The single was so easy to do and incredibly fun to put together – and people seem to really like it. Obsessive even!

RC: **Tell us about the album *Interplanetary Class Classics*, and do you write collectively?**

A: After the initial success of the first single, Dean and I wrote a load of new tunes, then Lias moved to Sheffield for the summer and we worked with him on lyrics and vocals. On a couple of songs, he had a few lyrics already written in his tatty old sports bag that worked with some of the tunes we had down. On other tracks, Lias and I would just bounce lyrics between us, or come up with daft concepts in the pub. Once we had another four or five tunes down with vocals and lyrics, we'd get Saul up for a day or so and he'd put down some pretty solid swampy guitar lines and backing vocals.

Once I had the main body of all the electronic drums and synths, organs, guitars, bass and vocals down, we took the parts to Sean Lennon's studio in New York and just beefed everything up with live drums and some unusual instruments he has there. The only song that came originally from Lias and Saul, and Nathan, was 'I.D.S.', which was a Fat White's song that wasn't quite working for them, which we turned into something more pumping and electronic.

RC: **Tell us about your relationship with Sean Lennon?**

A: Sean has been great to us. He helped us realise our wonky pop vision and brought lots to the table in the studio. He's a great all-round musician and as equally bonkers as the rest of us. He's got a north of England sense of humour, so he just gets us. He's a good mate.

RC: **You've been quoted as saying you "don't give a fuck about the music industry". Please explain?**

A: It's an industry that wants so much from you but gives you so little for your effort. For instance, we write and record a great album filled with catchy but weird singles that have already done the business on the radio. On top of this, meet unreasonable deadlines for artwork, whilst touring, doing interviews, making and coming up with concepts for videos, doing radio edits for singles, writing and answering loads of emails and smashing it out of the park live, selling out shows up and down the country. Pre-release, we received almost blanket critical acclaim for the album – and for what? . . .

For the distributor of our record to totally under stock shops on release day! It came out on a Friday and by the Saturday all the vinyl had sold out across the UK. This meant serious momentum was lost as it took four weeks to be re-pressed! There were barely any CDs to be found either.

On day one of release, it went to number 31 in the official UK charts; by day two, there were no records left in the shops. Even people who pre-ordered their records four months earlier had to wait for the repress, which is really bad for business and something that we were powerless to do anything about, so fucking our fans around pissed us off too.

That cock-up alone probably cost us a Top 20 album, which for us as a group working our arses off is a tragedy, because you want to be able to say to yourself that all the work we put in was worth it – and to temporarily make your family and friends believe you're less of a waster than they originally thought. Also, being a Top 20 group increases the chances of getting paid properly.

In short, I think they vastly underestimated the popularity of The Moonlandingz, and to me it showed a great lack of faith in the project. It has left quite a bitter taste in our mouths. I've worked far too hard not to take these kind of incredulous halfwit mistakes seriously!

SOMETIMES
Joseph Ridgewell

Sometimes
You encounter
Another human being
So
Repugnant
Odious
Loathsome
Disgusting
Sickening
And frankly repellant
That all you want to do
Is kick their fucking head in.

THE TRUTH WALKS ALONE
Gary Lammin

The truth walks alone
I bet that justice does too
And the distance between?
That's up to you
The world keeps turning
By hook or by crook
And the truth walks alone
That's how it's starting to look
The truth walks alone
Fiction crumbles to dust
That's how it should be
Once it's all sussed
The world keeps turning
By hook or by crook
And the truth walks alone
That's how it's starting to look

ACKNOWLEDGEMENTS

To the commitment and friendship of the close-knit Razur Cuts team: Dickson Telfer and Andrew & Gillian Gardner. An honest and trustworthy group who've never let me down. Love and thanks.

To the inspiration of: Scott T. Steel, Gordon Whyte, Fraser Houston, Stevie Wilson, Ally Gemmill, Doogs Mackie, Raymond Gorman, Jim Bowe, Chew Myles, Gordon Profit, David Ross, Neil Hodge, Colin Steer, Caroline Binnie, Trevor McPake, Sean from Memorial Device, Ian Cusack, Chris Quinn, Ali J, David Kidd, Martin Appleby, Swin P, John King, Steve Wright, Jason Williamson, Claire Herron Williamson, Davie Coutts, Colin Muldoon, Grant McNab, Gerry Mahoney (dummy), Coco J. Whitson, Paul Research, Martin Geraghty, Michaela and Cam Hunter, Gordon Tosh, Kevin Tosca, Danny Coyle, John Welsh, Danny Mac and Colin Meek – thanks so much.

To Joe England, who took the rudder to steer us on the proper course – indebted, mate.

To the artistic genius of: Suky Goodfellow, Tam Main, Carolina Russo, Hendo, Debs Mullen and Marcel Herms for agreeing to do front/back cover artwork in their own valuable time – much love.

Special thanks to stonedart for all his ongoing work to enhance our mag. A team member invite is in the post!

To my wife Annie and daughter Jenn – thanks for putting up with all things Razur Cuts over the last five years. Be prepared for more! Big love x.

To each and every one of you who believed in us by stocking, purchasing or contributing to the mag, and/or attending our gigs – massive thanks.

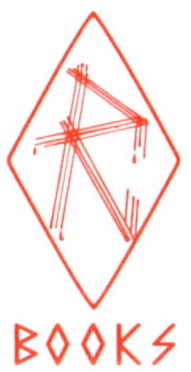

BOOKS

@razurcutsmag